the friendship Matchmaker

the friendship Matchmaker

Randa Abdel-Fattah

Walker & Company
New York

First published in Australia in 2011 by Omnibus Books, an imprint of Scholastic Australia
Published in the United States of America in July 2012
by Walker Publishing Company, Inc., a division of Bloomsbury Publishing, Inc.
www.bloomsburykids.com

For information about permission to reproduce selections from this book, write to
Permissions, Walker BFYR, 175 Fifth Avenue, New York, New York 10010

Library of Congress Cataloging-in-Publication Data
Abdel-Fattah, Randa.
The friendship matchmaker / Randa Abdel-Fattah.
p.   cm.
Summary: Lara Zany is her middle school's official Friendship Matchmaker,
but a new student, Emily Wong, has her own ideas on the subject and they
vie to match two "hopeless cases" with their perfect best friend.
ISBN 978-0-8027-2832-6
[1. Interpersonal relations—Fiction. 2. Friendship—Fiction.
3. Middle schools—Fiction. 4. Schools—Fiction.] I. Title.
PZ7.A15892Fri 2012   [Fic]—dc23   2011031428

Book design by Yelena Safronova
Printed in the U.S.A. by Quad/Graphics, Fairfield, Pennsylvania
2 4 6 8 10 9 7 5 3 1

To Monica,
for the licorice straps, sleepovers,
and "deep and meaningfuls"

the friendship Matchmaker

THE FRIENDSHIP MATCHMAKER MANUAL

BY LARA ZANY

WELCOME TO MY MANUAL.

My name is Lara Zany, and I am an official Friendship Matchmaker.

If you're reading this Manual it's probably because you're sick and tired of feeling lonely. Or maybe you have a friend but you're not sure where you stand with him or her. Or maybe you're the third wheel in a trio. Or can't work out how to strike up a conversation with somebody in the cafeteria line. Maybe you're the one who gets picked last for sports.

Don't worry. I'm here for you. You've come to the right place!

The first thing is to ignore every piece of advice your parents and teachers have given you. Look at them. They're old. They can't remember what it was like to be young. They believe in things like "being true to yourself" and "being accepted for who you are."

That stuff gets you beaten up.

The world of friendship matchmaking is complicated, and only a truly gifted person with a heart of gold can take it on. We're all given special talents and a reason to be in this world. I was made for this job. A lot of sacrifices have had to be suffered. A lot of hard decisions have had to be made. But I accept that. It's just the kind of person I am.

In my quest to make sense of school and help others make and keep friends, I've created a glossary of words to help you through my Manual.

GLOSSARY

BOBF	Bus Only Best Friend
BTFP	Bus Trip Faux Pas
FMM	Friendship Matchmaker
LBC	Loner by Choice
TL	Total Loner
MAK	Make and Keep
RFP	Reputation Faux Pas
FIMS	Friendship Intervention Mediation Session

— NOTE —

By the way, if you're reading this in Spanish or Turkish or Mandarin (which you probably are, given the book publishing deal I'm going to get), I want you to remember that it doesn't matter what country you live in or which language you speak. The Rules of school are the same all over the world.

There are those who survive.

And those who don't.

So read on to find out how to survive . . .

RULES FOR
THE FIRST DAY
OF SCHOOL

Follow these Rules if you're fresh blood. (I use the word "blood" on purpose. Schools are bloodthirsty war zones, and if you think I'm making this up you ARE a TL [Total Loner] and deserve to have no friends.)

1. Get rid of anything that can be used to tease you. That means you need to smell nice, brush your teeth, wear clean clothes, don't let your mom give you a weird haircut. Don't give people ammunition. (I told you this is a war zone.)

2. For those who wear glasses, are cross-eyed, have birthmarks in strange places, are too short, too tall, too skinny, or too

fat—you need to enter the war zone like officers in an army. You need extra protective gear. HOMEWORK: Think of every possible way you can be teased. Write a list. Then think up some great comeback lines. Be prepared, or be prepared to suffer.

3. For heaven's sake don't stand back waiting for somebody to talk to you. Everybody's looking for friends, and nobody's going to be interested in the weird kid who's sucking his thumb and looking like he's ready to vomit his breakfast on the floor. Walk up to people and start talking. BUT choose your conversation openers wisely.

Example of a good opener: "I saw (insert hottest movie star of the moment here) at the mall on the weekend, and he commented on how I have just the right look for his next (insert blockbuster movie)."

Example of a bad opener: "I'm so excited that we're learning long division this year."

You might have noticed that I am encouraging you to bend the truth.

This is SCHOOL, not church, temple, synagogue, mosque, or any other place of worship of your choice.

There's nothing holy about the cafeteria.

Chapter 1

I stood at the Potts County Middle School front steps with my Manual tucked under one arm and a clipboard under the other. The morning bell hadn't rung yet, and the courtyard was filling up on the first day of school.

I was ready. I'd spent the last week of summer vacation adding some new chapters to my Manual and changing some earlier ones. My mediation sessions had made me rethink a few strategies, especially in the Rules for Field Trips chapter.

Suddenly, I felt a tap on the back of my arm and turned around. A boy, probably in fifth grade, stared up at me.

"Excuse me, are you Lara Zany?"

I nodded.

"So you're . . ." The boy hesitated.

I knew exactly what he wanted to ask. And I was very pleased with his respectful, adoring look, so I flashed him a big smile.

The boy started again. "Are you Lara Zany, the one and only Friendship Matchmaker?"

Boy, did I love hearing those words.

"Yes, I am."

The boy sighed with relief. "My name is Dean. I'm new. They said I should come to you. Can you help me?"

I leaned down and looked the boy in the eye.

"Dean," I said, taking out my clipboard and scribbling his name on a notepad, "I'm Potts County Middle School's official Friendship Matchmaker, and I'm here to help. Now, let's get started. Tell me everything about yourself, and I'll find you the right friend in no time."

By the time the bell had rung, I'd matched some new kids in the fifth grade (Sophia and Hannah—loved ponies and enjoyed chocolate-covered peanuts; Dean and Zak—both sports obsessed; Naj and Edward—enjoyed collecting insects and soil samples) and scheduled a FIMS (Friendship Intervention Mediation Session) for recess between Marisol and Rachel from the sixth grade, who had been best friends until Rachel found a new best friend over the summer.

I made my way to the seventh-grade lockers. My classroom was open so I went inside and found a seat at the front. I put my pencil case on the desk and took out my exercise book covered in fluorescent-pink paper. My Top Secret Friendship Matchmaker Manual was tucked safely in the tray under my desk.

I glanced around the classroom and grinned. Everybody was either in a pair or foursome. Of course, I'd been responsible for matching most of the friends in the room. Except for Bart Franklin and Joseph Took, who had met at their Saturday karate classes—something told me they would eventually need me, though. The two only had karate in common. They'd soon realize that they couldn't talk about black belts six hours a day without eventually using the moves on each other.

I sat alone, but I preferred it that way. Nobody

dared to think I was a TL (Total Loner). I was an LBC (Loner by Choice). I'd made that very clear in all my pep talks and FIMS, and I knew that the general school population regarded me as the coolest and smartest seventh-grader around.

The only problem being an LBC was that for some dumb reason our teachers were obsessed with "group work" and making "team efforts." I'd tried to reason with Ms. Pria, but she simply refused to see my logic when it came to group activities or teamwork. I'd much rather work on my own, but if people chose to sit next to me in class or paired up with me for class work, I let them. Sometimes it couldn't be helped, and anyway, I've always had a heart of eighteen-carat gold.

Sometimes I'd pair up with a TL in class. I wasn't able to help everybody. Some people continued to be TLs in spite of all the effort I put into helping them make friends. That's because they didn't follow the Rules detailed in my chapter So You Have a Friend? Don't Be Too Confident! Learn How to Make and Keep Them.

I mean, you can take a donkey to water and make it drink, but you can't force it to burp, or whatever that saying is.

I made sure that the TLs knew I didn't have time for friends. I was in the business of helping *other people* make friends.

I sat quietly, waiting for Ms. Pria to arrive. Being the school's official Friendship Matchmaker had certain responsibilities, and I had to set an example. After all, most people wanted to be like me. If I was burping the national anthem like Chris, or making paper planes out of the pages of my notebook like Ralph, I'd probably start a trend. So I had to always be on my best behavior. It could get tiring, but when you have a heart like mine the sacrifices are easier to put up with.

The classroom was buzzing with noise as everybody swapped stories about their summer.

Everybody knew Ms. Pria was the best of the seventh-grade teachers. Rumor had it that Mr. Laidlaw picked his nose and wiped it on your textbook when he thought you weren't looking. And Ms. Simeon was obviously off in the clouds. So really that just meant Ms. Pria was the best of the worst.

While I waited patiently, I thought about the morning's events. The first days of school are always my busiest. New kids, kids transferred from other schools, kids whose best friends had dropped them in favor of a new best friend during the summer, were all begging me to help them. So already I'd sorted out a number of friendship pairs and foursomes.

(I have a strict policy against trios but the reasons for this are too disturbing to talk about just yet.)

This morning had been busier than usual, and I'd been forced to put off some FIMS requests. There had been a lot of best-friend swapping over the break. But the new kids who'd transferred from a nearby school had to take priority.

Finding a friend for one of them, David, was going to be a personal challenge for me. The kid clearly had issues, judging from the way he talked to his basketball.

Ms. Pria walked in. "Good morning, class," she said, with the same enthusiasm as somebody entering a lion's den. "I hope you're all looking forward to another year of learning. We're going to start with English this morning. I want you to break into teams of three and do the comprehension exercise I'm about to write on the board."

I couldn't believe it. A group project already? I raised my hand, annoyed with Ms. Pria.

"Yes, Lara?" Ms. Pria said.

I placed my hands on my lap and flashed her my winning smile. "Ms. Pria, could we please do the exercise alone?"

"No," Ms. Pria said and turned back to writing on the board.

I sighed patiently. Ms. Pria really didn't understand anything and needed the obvious to be explained to her.

"But, Ms. Pria, how can we do our best in a group when everybody's at different levels?"

"Lara Zany, it's called *teamwork*!"

I could not believe that it was only 9:03 a.m. and Ms. Pria had already lost her temper.

Tanya Zito, late on the first day, entered the classroom quietly and plunked her books down onto the desk.

Tanya was a Total Loner. Last year I'd tried, through many Induction Seminars, to help her. I'd warned her that people didn't like her obsession with sniffing school supplies before she used them (she especially liked rulers). But by the end of the year I'd added Tanya to my secret Terminal TL list and moved on to other more hopeful cases.

So when Tanya sat down next to me and started sniffing my pencil case, I tried with all my might to control my temper. Ms. Pria had already lost it. Somebody needed to set a good example.

I started to copy the passage on the board.

"You need to copy it, too," I told Tanya, who had moved on to sniffing a pink highlighter.

Just then the classroom door was flung open. The seventh-grade coordinator, Mr. Smith, walked in, followed by a girl.

"Ms. Pria," Mr. Smith said, "this is your

new student, Emily Wong. Class, be sure to make Emily feel welcome."

For some reason I locked eyes with Emily.

Immediately I knew this girl would be trouble.

Chapter 2

Ms. Pria told Emily to sit with me and Tanya. Our desk was big enough for three.

Emily pulled up a chair beside me and took out an exercise book. I noticed she had painted her fingernails black and white on one hand, and multicolored with glitter on the other. I took pity on the new girl and decided to offer her some free advice.

"You should wipe off your nail polish when you get home."

Emily scoffed. "Why?"

The poor thing. She really had no clue. "Because you'll just attract attention to yourself. It looks weird."

I went back to my copying. I'd hit the nail

on the head and was sure Emily would be asking the principal for nail polish remover at lunchtime.

But she just stretched out her hands and looked at her fingers. "Well, in that case, I'll keep the nail polish on a little longer."

I gasped. "I don't think you get what I'm saying," I said with a frown. Maybe she needed things explained several times. "You'll probably be teased."

"Because of my nail polish?"

I looked Emily up and down. "Well, now that you mention it, you shouldn't wear a Dora hair tie; that's for toddlers. And you shouldn't wear dolphin earrings; they're just so *girly*."

I was confident she would understand my wisdom. After all, my Fashion Rules were the most requested topic at my recess seminars.

"My cousin made me promise I'd wear her Dora hair tie on my first day of school," Emily said without a hint of embarrassment. "She's four. She said a fairy had given it to her as a good luck charm and that I had to wear it. Cute, huh? So I promised her. And I like dolphins, so I couldn't care less what people think about my earrings."

I couldn't believe my ears. I tried to think straight. Promises to four-year-olds? Cartoon-inspired dress choices in seventh grade? Dolphins? This was without a doubt the worst case of RFP (Reputation Faux Pas) I'd ever come across.

Not to mention that I'd never, *ever* been challenged before. I was the school's official Friendship Matchmaker. My word was law. People from all over the playground came looking for me, begging for a few words of wisdom. And when Harry Potter's publishers agreed to publish my Manual (it was nearly finished, just a few more chapters left), I'd be famous in schools all around the world. After all, being teased in an American playground was no different from being teased in a play-ground in England, China, or Norway.

So what screws were loose in Emily's head?

I was so annoyed that I looked at Tanya and snatched the pink highlighter out of her hand.

"Get a tissue and wipe your nose," I snapped. "It's covered in pink."

Rules for Lunchtime

1. Tell your mom to stop packing leftovers. They might taste like heaven but they're a RECIPE for disaster.
2. NO reading alone. But if you HAVE to, read next to somebody so you look like an LBC, not a TL. You do NOT want to be called a nerd. That label sticks like gum.
3. NO hanging out with the teacher on duty in the cafeteria, or the librarian, or any other grown-up. Trust me on this one. There's no turning back from a reputation as the teacher's pet.
4. Playing sports with boys (if you're a girl) or with girls (if you're a boy) is fine as long as you're not the only boy/girl. Possible names

you will be called: tomboy and sissy. Again, those labels stick forever.

Don't say I didn't warn you.

Chapter 3

At recess I held my FIMS between Marisol and Rachel in the small courtyard near the vending machines. There was an audience of loyal kids who had all benefited from my help matching them with other kids. Marisol and Rachel said they didn't mind.

I sat in the middle of a bench, clipboard in my hand, my Manual safely stored in my bag. Marisol sat on one side of me, Rachel on the other.

"Okay, Marisol, how about you start, since you're upset. Rachel, please don't interrupt until Marisol has finished. What happened?"

Marisol looked shyly at her audience, who

were munching on their chips and apples and cookies and watching Marisol like people at the movies.

"Well, Rachel was my best friend last year. We promised we'd be best friends forever, but we said if one of us went to another school or another state it was okay to get a new best friend. But if we stayed here then we had to be best friends forever and ever."

She paused and I gently coaxed her, saying, "Go on."

Rachel wriggled a bit.

"Well, on the first day of summer my mom said I could invite Rachel over to my house and so she called Rachel's mom who wasn't there so she spoke to Rachel's sister and asked her but her sister said Rachel had gone to the movies with their neighbor. So Mom said okay, what about that night? And Rachel's sister said Rachel was . . ."

The crowd leaned in. I moved closer. "Don't be nervous."

Marisol's voice was a whisper. "Sleeping over at her neighbor's place . . ."

The crowd immediately started muttering and making angry noises.

"A *sleepover*?" I asked.

Marisol nodded and then sniffed.

Ouch. The situation was worse than I first thought.

"Hmm, okay, and then what happened?"

"I didn't see Rachel for the rest of the summer. Every time we called to invite her over she was busy or out with Kelly, her neighbor. I don't know what I did wrong . . ."

"Okay, thanks for that, Marisol." I turned to face Rachel. "Rachel, what would you like to say?"

"I'm still Marisol's best friend! But my mom and dad were working, and my sister, who is mean, wouldn't drop me off anywhere. I got so sick of staying home all day that I played with Kelly next door."

Marisol sat up straight, listening intently.

"And the sleepover?" I asked grimly.

"It was Mom and Dad's anniversary and they were going out and my sister was going out and my aunt couldn't babysit, so Mom and Dad let me stay at Kelly's house. It was only the one time and it wasn't even fun. I mean, Marisol, you wouldn't believe it but Kelly doesn't even like drawing. She just wanted to watch TV."

"She doesn't like drawing?" Marisol repeated, looking horrified.

"Nope. *And* she fell asleep at nine o'clock."

"Nine?" Marisol shook her head in astonishment. "What a baby!"

"Yeah. Our sleepovers are *so* much better."

I interrupted. "Marisol, why didn't you ask to speak to Rachel? You could have explained how you felt and worked it out."

Marisol shrugged. "Because I thought she had a new best friend, so there was no point."

I turned to Rachel. "Why didn't you call Marisol during the summer?"

"I tried a couple of times but the machine picked up. I figured she was out having fun, so I didn't call again."

"Well, can you see that it was just a misunderstanding and that you're still best friends?"

They both nodded eagerly and stood up

to give each other a quick hug. The crowd cheered.

I uncrossed my legs and sat up straight.

"Okay, everybody. The lessons from today's FIMS are, first, when you're upset with your friend, talk about your feelings—that way things won't seem so confusing. Two, if you have a horrible sister or brother, find their diary or look up the text messages on their cell phone and blackmail them so they do what you say. Session dismissed."

Marisol and Rachel skipped off. I stood up, feeling happy that I'd saved another friendship from disaster. As I slung my backpack on my shoulder I noticed Emily Wong standing at the edge of the courtyard looking over my way.

I wondered why she had a grin on her face.

Rules for the School Bus (Part 1)

1. If you take the same bus to and from school every day you're probably stuck with the same people. They might not be in your class and you might ignore one another when you cross paths at school. But that's cool because you're Bus Only Best Friends.

2. Always prepare interesting conversation topics for your BOBF: "Did you see what happened last night on (insert mutually favorite TV show here)?"

3. Bring props like an iPod, if you have one, with earphones to share, Nintendo DS, or magazines.

4. Pack quality junk food (don't be tempted to eat it at recess or lunch). Everyone's

starving after school, so no healthy stuff
UNLESS your buddy is a health nut, in which
case offering junk food is a BTFP (Bus Trip
Faux Pas).

5. And, above all, always be ON GUARD!
   Keeping a friend is harder than making one.
   Remember the Make and Keep Rules (see
   later chapters for more details).

Chapter 4

I usually sit alone on the school bus. But when a TL needs a spot I'm okay with them sitting next to me as long as they don't expect me to become their best buddy.

Everybody knew that I was too busy sorting out other people's friendships to have time for friends of my own. (What they didn't know was what had led to me becoming the Friendship Matchmaker, but the reasons for this are too disturbing to talk about just yet.)

On my way to school the following week I sat next to Fred Dudley, grade six, whose usual BOBF (Bus Only Best Friend) was sick. He didn't have a backup so he needed me.

Fred was happy to read his book while

I worked on my Manual, putting my glossary in alphabetical order, which I thought would impress Harry Potter's publishers.

It had been a week since school started and I couldn't get Emily Wong out of my head. I'd noticed her at lunch on her first day, already breaking three Rules.

She'd been alone.

She'd been eating home-cooked leftovers.

And she'd been reading a book (and it wasn't even about fairies or vampires, which might have made it okay).

I really did pity her. Everybody knew that you didn't spend the first recess of your first day at your new school by yourself, eating smelly food and reading a book. There were so many options for the bullies. It would be brutal.

And then there was the horrible scene outside class. We had to all line up in front of the classroom and Emily had been singing along with her iPod—to the SpongeBob SquarePants theme song, in fact.

And the more people laughed, the louder she sang.

31

How could Emily possibly recover from that? Who would be her friend now? I tell you, I had a duty. Emily had so damaged her chances of social success that even the school counselor couldn't help her now. I was the only person qualified to fix this before it was too late.

So out of the goodness of my golden heart I decided then and there that I'd ignore Emily's obvious mental problems and offer her a double-session induction seminar. I checked my calendar and shuffled my appointments. Adam, Edward, John, and Todd's lunchtime FIMS would have to move to tomorrow. (The foursome had stopped talking after a fiery basketball game. Which, incidentally, was strange because they'd all been on the same team.)

The bus stopped at the next house. Toby, from fifth grade, hopped on. He approached a seat but another boy moved over, blocking him from sitting down. Toby looked like he was going to cry.

I noticed Fred's book, *A Complete Guide to Ponds*. I remembered Toby liked frogs. So

I stood up and told him to sit in my spot next to Fred.

It was moments like these that I understood why I was put on this earth.

Sitting behind Fred and Toby, by the time the bus arrived at school, I thought I'd heard everything I ever needed to know about ponds and frog spawn. I raced over to the seventh-grade corridor. I couldn't wait to meet Emily and tell her the good news before the bell rang for assembly.

But when I arrived I couldn't believe my eyes. She was surrounded by two girls, Claire and Jemma.

They were all laughing.

With Emily.

Not *at* her.

Then they linked arms and went off to the assembly area.

I was crushed.

Never had this happened before.

New kids needed me.

New kids with Dora hair clips who read alone at lunchtime and sang the SpongeBob

SquarePants theme song did not make friends by themselves.

They needed an induction session with me first.

They needed to have the Rules explained to them.

They needed to be trained and prepared for battle.

They did not, within days of school starting, find two friends all by themselves.

I sat on the floor in the corner of the locker area.

Horrible thoughts began to fill my head. What if Emily started a trend? What if others caught on? What if . . . I was no longer needed?

The bell rang. My stomach felt funny. I walked slowly to assembly.

Chapter 5

I just couldn't understand Emily. Maybe finding two friends by herself was a fluke. I watched her carefully during assembly.

She was wearing a T-shirt with a picture of a Barbie doll stuffing her face with a massive piece of cake and the words: "Get real, Barbie."

Dora one day, Barbie the next.

Also, she stood still and listened to the principal talking at assembly while Claire and Jemma whispered to each other. This was another mistake. It was a basic Rule of friendship groups: Never distance yourself from your friends, even when they are talking about something boring. You have to pretend to enjoy the conversation or you'll be kicked out of the group.

My head hurt from how obvious these Rules were! Only a TL would choose to ignore them.

Later, at recess, I overheard Emily tell Claire and Jemma that she'd "catch up with them later" because she was "dying to finish her book."

If it was a bestselling book about, say, vampires or fairies (which were on my List of Acceptable Books to Read in Public), I might have said okay. But it was a book about surviving in the wilderness. That was downright *crazy*. It would kill any hopes Emily had of fitting in and being liked.

The more I thought about it, the more worked up I got. It couldn't be helped that I was a very kind person. I took my role as Potts County Middle School's official Friendship Matchmaker *very* seriously. It was my duty to guide people, even ones who seemed to insist on being weird and different. On being *individuals*. That was a ticket to being a TL for the rest of your school life.

Emily needed me. Desperately.

Except the next day, before I could offer my

services, something weird happened that made me think she was beyond help. I'd dealt with all types. I was multiskilled. All kids just want to fit in.

But Emily seemed to be in a world of her own.

At lunchtime she sat at the bench near the lunch line with a big poster propped against the wall. It read:

ATTENTION!
Help raise money
for trampolines on the playground!
Don't use your allowance
to buy candy or juice;
donate your money to this *great* cause.
We want trampolines!
They will keep us healthy and maintain
the size of our jeans!
We'll forget computer games and
sitting on our butts!
Because we'll be too busy jumping
and having fun!
Only dollar bills accepted (or we'll be in
high school by the time we can afford them).

I approached Emily as several kids gathered and deposited their bills in the money box she was holding.

"Can you imagine how cool recess and lunchtime would be if we got some of those super trampolines?" she was saying. "And the teachers can't say it's unsafe with the nets they have now. We could have jumping competitions. I'd kick your butts! I'm excellent and my somersaults rock!"

The kids were cheering, and fighting to put their money in the box first.

When Emily saw me she flashed a smile and pointed to her poster.

"Want to donate?" she asked and made a loud pop with her chewing gum.

I was amazed and actually a little impressed. It took guts to have an opinion or get behind a cause at any time, let alone in the second week at a new school. Most kids, the kids who came to me for my top-quality help, would never dream of trying to stand out. But here was Emily, wearing rainbow tights and yelling at kids in the line to skip a meal and donate their money to her cause.

I stepped toward her and put two dollars in the money box. As Friendship Matchmaker, I have a responsibility to be kind to everybody, as troubled and disturbed as they might be.

"Thanks!" She beamed at me.

Then she raised her hands in front of my face. "Look, no nail polish today," she said with a grin. "Just Wite-Out. That's how I was able to draw the smiley faces. It dries and isn't as slippery as nail polish. Cool, huh?"

"Yeah, very cool," I said, with a look that indicated I thought she was a weird science specimen. "By the way, you shouldn't be listening to SpongeBob SquarePants on your iPod. Aren't you too old for him?"

She blew a bubble. "SpongeBob? What are you talking about?"

"I heard you the other day, singing a song about a pineapple under the sea."

Emily laughed. "I was listening to the top-twenty countdown but couldn't get that song out of my head from the night before. My cousin, the Dora hair clip one, is *obsessed* with that cartoon."

"Oh . . . well, try and avoid humming or singing toddler tunes. It's dangerous."

She gave me an odd look. I walked away quickly. It wasn't the ideal time to teach her these things. It looked like Emily was going to be in an altogether different category from my other projects.

RULES FOR SITTING AT TABLES

1. Round tables = GOOD. A circle means everyone is equal, so you're not left out.
2. Rectangular tables = BAD. If a rectangular table is the ONLY choice, try and sit in the middle. Don't hesitate to push people out of the way to get there. Never sit at the end of a rectangular table—you'll always be left out of the conversation and have to pretend to laugh at jokes you can't hear. Sitting on the end of a rectangular table is a TFP (Table Faux Pas).
3. Square tables = UNSURE. I am still developing a policy for square tables.

Chapter 6

During art, Ms. Pria broke the class into groups of four that she'd prepicked (all the TLs in the class sighed with relief).

I was grouped with Omar (who likes speaking in rhymes in training for his career as a rapper), Terry (who thought he was the best thing since sliced bread), and Emily (need I explain?).

Thankfully, the art room had round tables.

Each group had to make something out of papier-mâché. My group had to make a piggy bank.

"Piggy banks are dumb," Terry said as he started mixing flour and water for the papier-mâché paste.

"Why, pie?" Omar asked.

"Because nobody gets allowance in coins anymore. I get bills."

Emily wrinkled her nose. "You sound like a spoiled brat."

I was surprised. I didn't think Emily had ever spoken to Terry. How could she risk insulting him so soon? How did she know if Terry was the bully of the class or the most popular?

Enough was enough. I turned to Emily. "Could you help me get the newspapers from the supply room?"

"Sure."

"Get the sports page, cage," Omar called out.

I followed Emily to the supply room, closed the door, and faced her. "Emily, you're new here, right?"

She started picking up a pile of newspapers and then stopped, giving me a funny look. "Um . . . yeah . . ."

"Well, I'd like to offer you some friendly but professional advice. You're lucky. I normally do an induction session where I interview new kids and get all the data I need before giving out my expert tips."

I noted the dazed expression on her face and flashed her my winning smile. "Look," I said enthusiastically, "I'm here to help you!"

"Help me with what?" Emily replied, looking very confused.

I took a deep breath, trying not to lose my cool. My problem was that I cared *too* much. It had always been my weak point. "You're not going to survive school! You can't read by yourself at lunchtime! It might be okay if it's a bestseller, but even then it's better to be with your group! And you can't wear Dora hair ties and weird T-shirts with pictures of hungry Barbies on them! And you're lucky Terry is normally an okay boy! If he was Mr. Popular you would have lost your chances of him liking you by insulting him like that!"

I felt my face redden. I knew I was talking with exclamation marks. But I couldn't help myself. I went on. "This is what I live for! To help people like you who have no idea how to survive school! And you are doing *everything* against the Rules!"

"Why bestsellers only?"

I couldn't believe it. *This* was her response? I tried to calm down and reminded myself that Emily had brain problems and needed to be talked through this.

"Because bestsellers are cool and popular," I said, trying to disguise my annoyance at having to state the obvious.

She folded her arms across her chest. "So I should only read what's popular?"

"Well, at school, yes. At home you can read cookbooks or medical manuals if you like. But if you had done part two of my Induction Seminar you'd know that there's a big difference between how to act at home and how to act at school."

"Why? I think that's dumb."

My mouth dropped open. Everybody I'd ever helped had at least understood this Rule in a flash. And here was the new girl, arguing with me. "Because the Rules at home are different from the Rules at school," I explained. "You don't get teased by your mom and dad. The cafeteria is a war zone."

I wished I could refer Emily to chapter one

of my Manual, but I didn't want anyone to read it until Harry Potter's publishers had accepted it. I was imagining a book launch near the cafeteria where I'd hand out friendship bracelets with the Friendship Matchmaker logo (still in development) printed on them. But I was getting distracted . . .

"That's a pretty sad way to think of school," Emily said.

"Haven't you ever been bullied?"

"Lara, this is my *third* school. We've moved twice since I was in kindergarten. *Of course* I've been bullied."

"You've moved *twice*?"

That kind of track record was dangerous. No wonder she had no respect for my Rules. She was unsettled. Boy, did she need my help.

"Yep. First house we lived in was broken into twice so Mom insisted we move to another town, which meant changing schools."

"Oh."

"The burglars took a ton of stuff, including Mom's computer. But I was kind of glad because then we finally got an upgrade!" She giggled. "Don't tell her I told you that!"

"But why did you move again?"

"My grandpa died, so my nana moved in with us, but the house was too small. I've got triplet brothers."

"Lucky you."

"They're feral. So we had to find a bigger house, which meant changing towns *again*. New school, new bullies. Big deal. I've learned to handle them just fine."

This kind of confidence was disastrous. But she wasn't finished yet.

"I'm not going to change who I am just so I don't get bullied."

"But you have to. If you want to fit in and make friends you have to bend your personality a little bit." I wanted to say *a lot* but as I have a heart of gold I didn't want to hurt her feelings.

"Well, people who like me for who I am can be my friends."

Oh, boy. "That's how everybody starts,"

I said hotly. "And then they come running to me for help."

"I think you're giving people the wrong advice."

Oh no. Emily had gone too far now. I'd been polite but she'd pushed me to the limit.

"I can make anybody in this school popular and liked!" I cried. "I can give them friends and a future free from bullying and loneliness!"

"Yes, but they have to follow your Rules. Nobody can bring home-cooked lunches, only boring cheese sandwiches. There are no funny hairstyles. Everybody watches the same shows and likes the same TV stars. The girls read books about fairies, and the boys read books about superheroes. I saw a girl reading a book in the bathroom the other day because she was too scared to read it alone at lunchtime. You told her she'd be teased."

"But she would!"

"I met a girl named Maya who is dying to play soccer with the boys at recess, but you told her to stick with Natalie or she'll be teased for being a tomboy. Just because Natalie and

Maya have Russian mothers, you think they can be best friends."

"I didn't say that . . . I meant that they have enough in common to start to build a friendship . . . Look, my Rules work. The playground is a happy place here!"

Emily raised her eyebrows. "Prove it."

"What?"

"Prove that your Rules work."

Prove my Rules? I had a solid year of success behind me. I'd worked my fingers to the bone to help the school population make and keep friends. And now the new girl with her stupid T-shirt and dorky hair ties was telling me to prove myself?

Fine. I would show her.

"I'll take a Total Loner and find them a friend, a real friend. Then you'll see that my Rules work!"

"Okay. Well, I'll take a lonely person in the school and find them a friend, a real friend, but according to *my* Rules."

"Fine."

"Fine."

We stormed back to our table.

Omar looked at me. "Did you get my sports page, rage?"

For once his rhyme made sense.

Chapter 7

That night I sat on my bed and looked at my Terminal TL list. There were so many Total Loners to choose from in seventh grade.

I crossed out Kevin, who was number one on my list and who couldn't understand the difference between being a friend and being a stalker (he had a habit of going through people's bags).

I also didn't think David was going to get around to being normal any time soon. He was still talking to his basketball, and when I'd taken him aside at lunch yesterday for an Induction Seminar, he insisted that Bill, his basketball, also come along, as *it* was his best friend. I have sympathy for people who are best friends with objects (dolls, their comic book collection, computer games, their bike), but they have to understand that that sort of behavior has to stay at home. At school, friends need to have a heartbeat.

I eventually decided on Tanya. I was sure I could stop her school-supplies-sniffing habit. But she also needed a wardrobe makeover.

So I wrote down all the data I'd collected about Tanya.

ASSIGNMENT: FIND A FRIEND FOR TANYA (AND PROVE EMILY WONG WRONG)

PROFILE—TANYA

1. Sniffs school supplies. Especially rulers.
2. Wears hair in pigtails.
3. Wears weird clothes.
4. Tuesday is meatball lunch.
5. Terrible at all sports except maybe basketball.

6. Doesn't have anything to talk about. Just smiles or shrugs. Need to fill her head with conversation topics.

POSSIBLE FRIENDSHIP MATCHES

1. Julie. Apparently she has no sense of smell (see meatballs, above) and is good at basketball.
2. Carla. Wants to be a hairdresser when she grows up. Maybe she can practice on Tanya?
3. Lucy. Parents run a drug store. (Maybe not a good idea. Perfect access to school supplies.)
4. Stephanie. Most talkative kid in class. Can she make up for Tanya's silence?

Note to self: The most important thing is that the friendship is real and lasts. Remember the most important Friendship Matchmaker Rule: MAK (Make and Keep)!

I put my notebook on my bedside table and laid my head on my pillow. Before a friend could be matched to her, Tanya needed a makeover. Tomorrow would be the beginning of some serious training sessions. Not since the time that led to me becoming the Friendship Matchmaker (still too disturbing to talk about) had I been so determined to get something right. All other friendship crises in the school would have to go on hold while I dedicated all my efforts to proving Emily wrong.

My reputation as Potts County Middle School's Friendship Matchmaker depended on it.

Chapter 8

By the end of the week Emily had collected almost two hundred dollars toward trampolines for the playground. Her fund-raising efforts came to a stop when Mr. Smith stormed into our classroom after lunch on Friday.

"Ms. Pria, are you aware that Emily Wong has been collecting money from students?"

Ms. Pria looked over at Emily in surprise. "No," she said.

"I've had kids falling asleep from hunger in the afternoon because they've donated all their lunch money to fund-raising for trampolines!" Mr. Smith was furious. "Not to mention that the cafeteria has been in an uproar. They're barely breaking even. Almost no students are buying lunch."

"Is this true, Emily?" Ms. Pria said. "Did you get permission from the principal?"

"No," Emily said with a shrug. "I didn't think I had to. Sorry."

Ms. Pria sighed and rubbed her temples. "Well, did you keep receipts?"

"Receipts?" Emily grinned. "'Course not. Why would I give someone a receipt for a dollar? It's not really worth the effort."

Mr. Smith's face was turning bright red. "Then how on earth will we return all the money? We have no idea how much each child donated!" He turned to Emily. "Young lady, this is not how we do things at this school. You can't just take money from children without permission."

"But I had their permission," Emily said.

Someone called out, "She's got you there!" And the class burst into laughter.

"Don't be sassy!" Mr. Smith said. "I mean a *teacher's* permission."

In the end Emily was sent to the principal's

office to explain. Mr. Muñoz was actually a big softie. The real person to steer clear of was the assistant principal, Ms. Annabelle, but she was on vacation, so Emily was lucky. And because it was too hard to work out how much money was owed to whom, the school decided to add the money Emily had collected to the playground equipment budget and sent explanatory letters home. Emily was disappointed we weren't getting trampolines but happy that the money was at least going toward play equipment.

She'd only just started at our school and was already one very popular girl.

I felt like I was losing control. Nobody had ever claimed fame without my help in some way.

I didn't like the situation one bit.

Chapter 9

Chris was the seventh-grade bully. Actually, make that Bully, with a capital B. I noticed him on my way to class on Monday morning. He was ripping a magazine into tiny pieces, letting them fall in front of cowering Kevin's eyes.

I walked straight up to Chris and yanked the torn magazine out of his hand.

"Don't be such a jerk," I yelled.

"What's it to you?" he shouted back.

I wondered if I should bother explaining the common bond between human beings in the fight against evil.

Chris put his face up close to mine and flipped his eyelids.

On second thought, I didn't think there was any point.

"Betcha can't do that!" he cried.

"Why on earth would I want to?"

Chris flipped his eyelids back.

I handed Kevin the remains of his car magazine. He sniffed, thanked me, and walked away.

"You think you're so good," Chris said with a sneer.

"Well, when I think of you, I think of bug spray," I said calmly, and whirled around and walked away, running into Emily on my way to class.

"Have you found someone yet?" Emily asked.

"Yes," I said. "Let's meet at recess in the courtyard, and we'll go through the terms and conditions of the contest. Have you found someone?"

"Yep!"

We stared at each other for a moment and then parted.

That's when I noticed the words on the back of her T-shirt: Rules Are Made to Be Broken.

I took this to mean the war was going to be very personal.

I hurried to the classroom and found Tanya sitting alone sniffing her calculator. I slid in beside her and arranged my things on the desk.

Tanya was so surprised she stopped sniffing. "You're sitting next to *me*?"

I grinned. "Tanya, today is your lucky day. I'm officially making you my Special Project. I'm going to find you a best friend. Are you with me?"

Tanya beamed. "Wow . . . I can't believe it. Why me?"

I didn't know how to answer that question without making Tanya cry. It was one thing to have her in the top five of my secret Terminal Total Loner list; it was another thing to tell her that. "Tanya, I really want to help you out. I know we've had some sessions before and they didn't go too well. So now I'm offering you my personal, one-on-one services. I'm cutting back on all my other duties. There will be a schoolwide crisis, but I'm here for you, and you alone."

"Wow. I mean, I'd love a best friend . . . it would be amazing . . ."

"You just have to promise to follow my Rules. And in return I promise that if you do, I'll find you a best friend."

"Okay," Tanya said, grinning. "Deal!"

Tanya went back to sniffing her calculator. I snatched it out of her hand. "Sorry, Tanya. The sniffing-school-supplies thing ends *now*."

Tanya looked embarrassed. "Oh. I didn't realize . . ."

"Yes, well, you do it a lot and it has to end. That is my first Rule."

Tanya nodded. "Okay, sure. I'll try."

"We'll meet at lunchtime today and go through all the Rules. I just have another private appointment at recess."

"So should I just do what I always do at recess?"

"What's that?"

"Help Mr. Thomas stack books in the library."

I tried not to cough. Could it really be *that*

bad? "Uh, for today only. I'll have a program for you starting tomorrow."

I turned around to look for Emily. She was sitting alone, sketching on her folder.

I wondered who her project was.

⌇

Bethany Faddy.

Was Emily kidding? I could see them waiting in the courtyard. I quickly looked up my TL list. Both our choices were from my top five TLs. Well, Emily and I were obviously suckers for hard work.

I skimmed through Bethany's profile.

PROFILE—BETHANY

1. SO MANY annoying habits. For example, no idea about personal space. Always close-talking.
2. Usually has bad breath. (See point no. 1 for why this is a problem.)
3. Doesn't believe in chewing gum, lollipops, or mints. (See point no. 1 again for why this is a problem.)
4. Environment crazy. All she talks about is

recycling and saving water and how paper
is evil and we should each have our own
blackboard and chalk.

5. Hates anything electronic: iPods, Nintendo
DS, all cell phones. Probably thinks we
should communicate using pigeons.

6. Vegetarian (okay, that can be cool) and
her family also doesn't believe in junk food.

7. Always lectures everybody. (See point
no. 4.)

I was annoyed that Emily had brought
Bethany to our meeting. It was unfair to
Bethany. I mean, why did she have to know
she was a guinea pig in our experiment? That
was cruel and something I would never do.
Emily obviously didn't even have a *silver* heart.
Hers was probably made out of aluminum.

I hid my Manual in my backpack and walked
up to them.

Bethany took a massive step toward me, her
nose practically touching mine.

"Hi, Lara!"

Definitely sour-cream-and-onion chips for lunch. Probably soy based. "Hi, Bethany."

"How are you?" she continued.

I tried to back away slightly, without making it too obvious. "I'm good. Do you mind if I talk to Emily alone for a moment?"

Maybe I was speaking a different language, because Bethany completely ignored me and said, "I heard you talking with Daniel from the fifth grade the other day about his trip to Fiji with his parents. You were trying to find him a match. I went up to him afterward and told him he's lucky to be alive. Sea levels are on the rise, you know, and they could have been caught in a tsunami or just drowned in a high tide. That's what you get with global warming. He started crying. It's pretty good that he's so worried about the environment, isn't it?"

One thing was certain. I was going to win this competition! "Oh, that's great, Bethany. Convert them early."

"My mom and dad are thinking about suing the school because they don't sell organic food in the cafeteria."

Emily stopped Bethany then. She asked Bethany to fill her recyclable bottle of water from the fountain, because she didn't believe in the evil plastic bottles the cafeteria sold.

Bethany grinned and ran off.

"Okay," I started, taking control. "We need to talk about the details. I've chosen Tanya. You've chosen Bethany. How long do we have to find them a friend?"

"Well, seeing as you're the *expert*, you decide."

"A month. Do you think you can manage?"

"Huh!" she said, folding her arms. "Of course!"

"The friend has to be genuine. No recess or lunchtime buddies who ditch them when the bell rings." I leaned in closer, making sure she understood how serious I was. "We're talking *best friend* material."

Emily shrugged. "That's no problem."

We locked eyes for a moment and then went our separate ways.

Rules for the School Bus (Part 2)

1. While you're waiting for the school bus, there is absolutely no point in talking to somebody who already has a friend to sit next to. That is a Bus Trip Faux Pas (BTFP).

2. Also, don't be tempted by trios. A trio is an unstable, dangerous friendship unit that is totally incompatible with standard two-person bus seats.

3. If you sit next to the odd one in someone else's trio, don't think they will include you in their trio talk. You are just a butt on a seat because while trios can become a pair by killing off the odd one out (refer to chapter on trios), they will rarely become a foursome, so you WILL NOT CONVERT THEM.

Chapter 10

I took Tanya to a quiet corner of the school playground at lunchtime. I'd come with a half-finished can of styling mousse I'd snatched from my sister's room, and a summary of my FMM Fashion Rules, which I'd written out in class before lunch while Ms. Pria was reading aloud to us.

"Okay," I began. "Tanya, I want you to take my Fashion Rules home and study them. You need to try and fix your wardrobe. People like to be seen with trendy people. So no more track pants. From now on you're in jeans. And no more tops your grandma made for you with pictures of baby animals on them."

"My mom makes them for me," she said quietly.

"Okay, even worse. No more anything any family member makes for you."

"But Mom will be so upset," she whispered.

I lost my temper. It happens. Even to people with hearts of gold like me.

I shook her by the shoulders. "Do you want me to help you, Tanya?" I shouted.

"Yes . . ."

"Do you want to be lonely for the rest of school, or do you want somebody to play with every recess and talk to every lunchtime?"

"I want someone to talk to . . ."

"Do you want to stop worrying about whether you'll have someone to sit next to in class or on the bus? Look me in the eye and tell me you want all these things, Tanya. I'm the Friendship Matchmaker. I can change your life!"

I'd let it all out. I calmed down and smiled. Maybe my hopeful face would rub off on her.

She sniffed. "Yes, I want all that . . . badly . . ."

I gave her a quick hug. "Okay! Then trust

me. If it upsets your mom that much, wear her sweater on the way to school, then stash it in your bag. Honestly, I think it should be illegal for a school not to have a uniform. I mean, it would make my job so much easier. Do you know how many training sessions I run because people get bullied for their fashion sense?"

Tanya shook her head.

"Never mind, you don't need to worry about that. Okay, so study my notes and your clothes will be fixed. Next: hair."

"My dad says he loves my curls," she said, patting her wild hair, "because I look exactly like my mom except for my hair. Which is like his."

I rolled my eyes. "That's sweet. But your dad's not here with you when Chris calls you Electric Shock, is he?"

The expression on her face told me she wasn't convinced. She was harder work than I thought.

"Look, your curls are really nice, but to be honest—and I say this only because I'm trying to help you—you look like you've been camping in the woods and just woke up."

"Oh . . . okay . . ."

"So you have some options. I brought you some mousse. It's my sister's. Put it in your hair to stop it from standing up like that, or pull your hair back. Look, I'm not a control freak. I'll leave it up to you. Just make sure you bring extra elastic bands tomorrow so I can change it if I don't like it. Cool?"

She agreed and I ticked "hair" off my list.

"Some other Rules," I continued. "No meat-balls for lunch. Ever. They may be yummy but they stink, and stinky food is a one-way trip to being bullied. Got it?"

"Yep."

"Can you play basketball? The other day I heard you talking about how you play on the weekends."

"Well, yeah, I can dribble and shoot the ball."

"Are you good at it? Me? I'm hopeless. So be honest with me."

"Well . . . yeah, I'm okay. I'm a good shooter.

Dad plays ball with me at the park near his house when I visit him."

I looked down at my list but out of the corner of my eye I noticed she seemed a bit upset. Maybe she'd had enough for one day. Not everybody could keep up with me.

"Okay, look, let's finish the training session now. That's enough for you to digest."

"Great, thanks so much, Lara. You really are the best kid in the school."

I smiled modestly. "Oh, thanks, Tanya. I just love to help. That's all."

That afternoon after school Julie was at the school bus stop. Her stop was before mine but it didn't matter. Even though my Rules said to sit next to someone who gets dropped after you, I was an LBC and was excused from the Rules.

Julie had her basketball tucked under her arm. I walked up to her and said hi. She looked happy that I was talking to her. Julie had a best friend (Lucinda) but she wasn't getting on the bus. Also, I think there were cracks in their friendship. Lucinda had told me secretly she was getting sick of basketball but didn't know how Julie would take it if she told her.

I thought maybe if I could get Tanya into basketball she might have a chance with Julie.

I just had to test the waters first.

"So, Julie," I said, "guess who I discovered is a crazy basketball fan too?"

"Who?"

"Tanya."

"School-supply-sniffing Tanya?"

I nodded. "Yep. Oh, and she doesn't do that anymore. It was just a medical condition, but she took pills for it and she's cured now."

Julie started dribbling the ball. She didn't seem excited by the news.

"So why don't you both hang out at recess tomorrow? Get to know each other. Maybe even shoot some hoops? She's amazing with the ball."

"Sounds good," Julie said, shrugging. "'But I've never seen her on the basketball court at recess or lunch."

"Well, she's never been invited. But that's not your fault. You didn't know she's a champion player."

I left it at that and arranged with her to meet us at the courts at recess the next day.

Chapter 11

In the evening I logged on to e-mail at home. My user name is FMM. I use e-mail for my out-of-school-hours Friendship Matchmaker services.

I had lots of messages from clients.

Wandmaker Hi, FMM, I'm in sixth grade. Jessica says she won't play with me on Wednesdays and Thursdays because Natasha is going to be her best friend on those days. What should I do?

Brickboy My best friend stinks at football. I didn't pick him in PE and he's angry. Do you think I was being unfair?

Tasha8 NO ONE WANTS TO PLAY WITH ME! HELP!

As I was going through the messages and responding, my big sister, Tara, came into my room and hovered over me.

"Chatting on e-mail?" she said. "Finally got a friend?"

"I'm working," I said.

She plunked herself down on my bed. "Don't be such a weirdo."

I turned to face her. "I don't have time for friends. I'm too busy helping other kids."

She raised an eyebrow. "That's dumb."

"You have so much to learn," I said impatiently. "I'm anything but dumb."

Her voice was suddenly tender. "Don't you get sick of being a loner?"

I rolled my eyes. "You wouldn't understand."

I imagined how Tara would react when Harry Potter's publishers contacted me with a book deal. The thought put a big smile on my face.

Tara stood up. "What happened to your friends from before? You three were glued at the hip."

"Go away!" I screamed.

Tara shook her head and left the room.

I sat very still for a moment. I tried to think happy thoughts.

My Manual on the shelves in bookstores.

Book signings all over the country.

When I'd calmed down I turned back to the computer and continued helping the kids who had e-mailed me.

Sometimes I thought I needed them as much as they needed me.

～

The next day I met Tanya outside our classroom. My heart of gold melted with pride.

Her hair was brushed back into a ponytail, and she was wearing a sparkly pink headband with matching pink earrings.

"I borrowed them from my cousin," she said shyly, when I asked her where she'd been hiding such gems.

She was wearing a pair of jeans (thank goodness, no track pants) and a plain white T-shirt with a cute pink collar. There wasn't a knitted furry animal in sight.

The best part was when she showed me her cheese sandwich.

"And it's not even the smelly kind!" she boasted.

I gave her a quick hug.

I walked into class with Tanya proudly at my side.

Chris saw her and yelled out, "What happened to you, Electric Shock?"

"Shut your trap!" I snapped at him. "At least Tanya doesn't wear the same underwear all week!"

I didn't know if that was true, but I guessed with a creep like Chris he'd be disgusting in every way.

Some of the class burst out laughing.

"I only change 'em on the weekends," he said and winked at the class.

"What a loser," I muttered to Tanya.

Ms. Pria was at her desk, holding a cup of tea. She ordered us to sit down quickly.

Emily was sitting next to Bethany. I made sure to lock eyes with Emily and tried not to look too happy with myself. But she just smiled at me, totally unaffected by Tanya's transformation.

To my delight, Bethany looked just the same. Emily hadn't bothered to give her a makeover. Bethany always dressed like she was going camping. She wore army-colored pants with heavy boots I'm sure she bought from the boys' section in the store, and hand-knitted cardigans in odd colors. Her hair was always in a million braids or else she bunched up sections of it into little buns all over her head.

She was a bully's dream.

Tanya and I sat down. I had to stick with her until I found her a friend.

Also, it was her first day as the new Tanya. She needed some extra support.

Ms. Pria started telling us about our math lesson. She jiggled her tea bag up and down in her cup and then took it out and threw it in the garbage.

Bethany's arm shot up. "Ms. Pria, you can't do that!" she shrieked.

"What are you talking about, Bethany?"

"You have to recycle the staples and little paper tag in the tea bags. That's what we do at home."

"What nonsense!" Ms. Pria scolded.

"But you have to!" Bethany said. "The paper and staple are recyclable. And you can reuse the tea bag."

Other kids in the class were groaning. I would have felt sorry for Bethany but I had to think of Tanya's interests. I stole a glance at Emily. Amazingly, she looked calm. She should have been panicking. Who will want to be Bethany's friend now? She was just so *obsessed*.

"That's enough, Bethany!" Ms. Pria yelled.

She was always losing her temper. I didn't think she liked being a teacher very much.

"This humble cup of tea is not going to ruin the world! Now, can I explain fractions to the class?"

"Yeah, go on, Ms. Pria," Toby called out. "We'd rather learn math than listen to Bethany go on about tea bags."

Some of the kids giggled.

What a disaster for Emily!

When the bell for recess rang and we were all putting our things away, Emily stood up and said, loud enough for most of the class to hear, "My uncle is an artist and he sews used tea bags together to make beautiful artwork. He's made thousands doing stuff like that."

"Wow. Really?'

"Just from used tea bags?"

"So Bethany was right . . ."

"Imagine getting rich from used tea bags!"

I noticed Bethany beaming as some of the kids crowded around her, asking for other ideas that would make them rich.

"But it's about saving the planet," Bethany argued.

Emily spoke up. "Well, if you can save the planet *and* make money, that would be awesome!"

Bethany smiled. "Yeah, that's true. And you could always donate your profits to a rainforest campaign."

I walked out of class quickly. Tanya followed me. Bethany was attracting a lot of good attention. How had she gone from being a weirdo to suddenly having a group of kids wanting to talk to her?

Emily Wong.

I'd underestimated her. She was better than I thought.

⁓

Okay. I exaggerated Tanya's ability to play basketball. She got the ball through the hoop *once*. And when she dribbled, the ball seemed to want to be anywhere but under her control.

Within ten minutes Julie was fed up.

"I thought you said Tanya was awesome?!" she yelled at me.

Tanya stood still but didn't say a word in her own defense.

"She is," I snapped back. "It just takes the right kind of teamwork. Come on, Tanya, let's go."

Lucinda, who'd also been playing, watched with sympathy. It was obvious she didn't want to keep playing, but Julie passed the ball to her and cried out with manic enthusiasm, "Come on! Let's play some *real* ball!"

Tanya followed me away from the courts.

"What happened? Didn't you say you were a good shooter?"

81

"Well, yeah, that's what Dad tells me all the time."

I groaned. It was my fault, not hers. I'd always made it a rule to never listen to compliments paid by parents. They were *supposed* to make their kids feel good about themselves. I'd had to sort out hundreds of problems caused by parents overpraising their children.

"Well, never mind," I said, giving her a reassuring pat on the arm. "There is plenty of other best-friend material out there. We'll keep on trying."

"Do we have to try now? Could we maybe just hang out for the rest of recess?"

I looked over at her. "Okay. We'll try again tomorrow. I need to prep you at lunch today. Our next target is Carla."

Tanya grinned. "Cool! So . . . I noticed you like writing."

"Yeah, I do. How'd you guess?"

"I see you writing in a book all the time. And then you put it away like it's something special. You always have a dreamy look on your face when you're writing."

I smiled. "I love it."

"Is it a diary?"

"Nah. I don't keep one."

"Me either. So what do you write?"

"It's private . . . sorry." Huh! Wouldn't she and the rest of the school like to know?

"That's okay. I write too, you know."

"*Really?* What do you write?"

"It's also a secret."

I laughed. "Two secret writers. Well, let's give each other a clue."

"Okay! My book is kind of like a how-to book. Like a long piece of advice."

"No way! So is mine. Well, it's more like a manual."

We laughed.

"So when do you write?" I asked.

"Mainly at night, before I go to bed."

"Same!"

We spent the rest of recess talking about our writing habits and who our favorite writers are and what we do when we get stuck for words. I confessed that I actually hate books about talking fairies and vampires but that at school they are really the only books that are cool to be seen reading. I explained that this was based on a year of research, and Tanya said she understood because I was the expert. Anyway, she also hates those kinds of books. Like me, she reads fantasy, horror, and action books. We swapped our lists of book titles, promising to read each other's favorites and report what we thought.

By the time the bell rang, I'd almost forgotten that I was supposed to be training Tanya on our next target, Carla.

It's okay, I thought. *We'll have all of lunchtime. Or maybe even half of lunch and the rest we could spend talking about our fantasy-book collections.*

Chapter 12

At lunchtime I gave Tanya all my tips on Carla. How she wanted to be a hairdresser and liked spending breaks doing braids and other nice things to people's hair. I explained that Carla was very sweet and easy to talk to. She didn't really like sports so there was no way Tanya would have to go through the basketball disaster again.

I'd slipped into my sister's room that morning and taken one of her hair magazines. She had a pile because she was trying to decide how to do her hair for her senior prom. She was way older than me and had lots of amazing magazines. I stole things from her room a lot, and she screamed at me when she found out.

The plan was to walk past Carla at lunchtime, with Tanya holding the hair magazine. She had to make sure Carla noticed.

Carla was standing on a bench behind a girl named Ayshe, playing around with Ayshe's hair. Tanya walked past them. I peeked around a corner within hearing distance.

Bingo. I was just *too* good.

Carla shrieked. "Wow! Tanya, is that the latest *Hair Catwalk Expo* magazine?! I've been saving all my allowance for that!"

Tanya looked at me and I waved my arms around, trying to get her to stop looking at me and focus on Carla.

"Um . . . yeah, it is . . ."

I tried to send mental messages to Tanya. *Be confident! Be confident!*

"Can I *please* take a look? It's, like, the best magazine in the world. Where did you get it?"

Tanya answered, just as we'd practiced.

"It's my friend's sister's magazine. She's a trainee hairdresser. She has them lying all around the house. She gave it to me because she knows I love hairstyles."

It was a teeny-weeny white lie. My sister was not a trainee hairdresser. She was still in high school. And like I said, I stole the magazine from her room. But sometimes you had to bend the truth if it meant beating Emily—I mean, finding Tanya a true friend.

But Tanya sounded like she was reading a script. She needed to loosen up, the way she was with me. Why couldn't she talk like that now?

Carla jumped off the bench, leaving Ayshe with wild hair all over the place. Tanya handed Carla the magazine. Carla grabbed Tanya's hand, sat her down beside her, and started flipping through the magazine, pointing out hairstyles.

"Look at this one! It's gorgeous! Ooh! Look at that one! Can you see how they've cut the back but left the front long? It's so different!"

"Yeah!" Tanya said, trying to sound excited. "The hairstyles are really nice."

Carla pressed the magazine to her chest and looked up at the sky. "One day I'll have hairstyles in a magazine too!"

"Um . . . yeah . . . imagine how cool that would be . . ."

"What's your dream?"

Tanya was prepared. "To, um, do hair for all the movie stars."

"Me too!" Carla laughed. "Wow! So do you think we should do an updo for Ayshe or leave it down? The updo shows off her eyes. But the down is more casual for school. What do you think?"

This was definitely *big* progress. Carla was asking Tanya for her advice. She was acting like they were a hairdressing team.

"Um . . . we could try both and see what looks better . . ."

"*Great* thinking!" Carla cried.

She leaped up onto the bench and started back on Ayshe's hair.

"Come on up," she told Tanya. "You can try it too."

A couple of moments later Emily and Bethany walked past. I couldn't help but point out Tanya and Carla, who were standing side by side on the bench, both working on Ayshe's hair. I flashed Emily a triumphant grin. She walked up to me.

"Since when does Tanya like hairdressing? I may be new but even I can guess it hasn't been her hobby for long."

"Well, some people pick up hobbies quickly."

Emily raised an eyebrow. "So you're changing the way she looks and what she likes, just so she'll make a friend."

"What's wrong with that?"

She raised an eyebrow again. "Hmm . . . nothing . . . See you around . . ."

Bethany and Emily walked off.

I was fuming. She was so stuck up. I *knew* what worked. And she was the new girl acting like I was some evil witch making people miserable!

Carla asked Tanya to sit next to her in class after lunch. She kept flipping through the magazine and asking Tanya what she thought about all the hairstyles.

Tanya had definitely won the toughest battle. Carla had invited her to sit next to her.

I was sure it was the beginning of an amazing friendship.

Meanwhile Bethany was still stuck like glue to Emily. Maybe Emily had missed the point. Emily was supposed to *find* Bethany a best friend, not *be* Bethany's best friend.

I said bye to Tanya and Carla after school and hopped on the bus. It'd been a great day.

Tanya called me that night and we spoke for half an hour. At first she told me all about Carla and how she was trying her best to become a hairstyling fan. It sounded like things were going really well. Carla had swapped phone numbers with Tanya and said she wanted to get friendship bracelets made out of braided horse hair. She thought human hair would feel a little icky.

Then we started talking about school and how English was our favorite subject. We talked about how we didn't really like Ms. Pria, but the librarian, Mr. Thomas, was the best teacher ever. I confided in Tanya that I wrote poetry and that my mom and dad liked to frame everything I wrote and hang it in the hallway. Tanya said she wrote short stories and used to read them to her parents and that they would staple them together into little books.

Chapter 13

Tanya came rushing up to me toward the end of recess on Friday.

"I can't talk about hair for one second more!"

My heart sank. Being as smart as I am, I instantly knew Carla was now out of the picture and we were back to square one.

"What's wrong?"

"I'm so sorry, Lara. I know you're trying really hard, but I can't stand hanging out with Carla. Honestly, I'd rather be alone."

"Don't say that!" I cried. It was worse than swearing.

"Since the bell rang this morning she hasn't stopped talking to me about the salon she plans to open when she's finished with school, and her favorite hairstyles, and which celebrity has the best color. I'm going crazy!"

I tried not to look too disappointed.

"I promise I will follow all your other advice, but don't make me stay with Carla. She came to school this morning with colored mousse. She tried to convince me that it will look great if I have rainbow curls! I just lost it and told her I hate mousse, hairspray, and perms. She was really upset."

"Okay, we'll try someone else . . ."

I thought back to my list of possible best friends for Tanya. The next person was Lucy. Even though her parents owned a drug store and she had the best pencil case collection in our class, I didn't think school supplies would be a problem anymore. Tanya seemed to have stopped sniffing rulers and paper clips.

"Let me think about how to pair you with Lucy . . . I think this calls for a Bungee Jump Friend attempt."

Tanya looked terrified. "Huh?"

"It's one of my best tricks. I save it for

special people. Instead of preparing you, I'll throw you into a conversation with Lucy and you have to bounce right into it. So it's up to you, okay? You don't have to learn any lines by heart, like you did with Carla, or try to play professional basketball, like you did with Julie. Just be yourself and talk to Lucy."

Tanya still looked terrified.

"It's okay," I said in the voice I used when I was helping pair off fifth-graders on their first day of school. "You'll be fine. Just remember there are some topics you *don't* want to mention. Do you want me to write them down for you? That way you can look at them when you're with Lucy. In case you get stuck."

"That would be fantastic."

I sat down and took out a piece of paper from my purse. I carried it with me for moments just like these. That is what you do when you live to help others at any minute.

When I finished, I handed her the list. It was just a quick pick from my more detailed Manual, which no one was going to see until Harry Potter's publishers accepted it.

TOPICS TO STAY AWAY FROM

1. Anything your parents talk about. For example, politics or bills or the environment.

2. Any health or medical problems you have (like itchy toes, warts, or lice).

3. What your parents think about you. For example, "My mom says I have a beautiful voice" or "My dad says I have the face of an angel."

4. Talking about how you love a teacher.

5. Talking about how you love schoolwork.

6. If you hate any popular singers or actors, just keep it to yourself. Some people love their celebrities more than their families and will have a meltdown if you disagree.

When Tanya finished reading the list she looked up and said, "Most of this is what *we* actually talk about."

I shrugged.

"Like how we don't like Justin Bieber.

And how we love creative writing in English. And how our parents think we'll be great writers one day."

"I told you, home and school are different. If you want to survive school, you have to come as a new person. It's fine for you to share that stuff with me. I'm the Friendship Matchmaker. I made the Rules, so I know the right time to bend them. And I would never bully you, so you're safe with me. But we're trying to find you a best friend. You won't know what she's really like until you're close to her. So play it safe at first. Okay?"

Tanya smiled. "Okay, Lara. Whatever you say. You know what you're doing. And honestly, I'm just so happy you chose to help *me* out of everybody."

"It's my duty, Tanya. I have a gift. I'd feel terrible if I didn't use it. Okay, we'll do Bungee Jump Friend at lunchtime. Try to relax and stay calm until then."

⌣

"I want you to get into pairs for your next lesson," Ms. Pria said.

I tried not to groan.

"I want you to design a project about the environment, because next Wednesday is our school's Save the Planet Day."

"Do we get the day off?" Jemma called out.

"No, Jemma, we obviously do not get the day off."

There was a collective moan.

"I want to see some enthusiasm! You've all just returned from summer break. A day off should be the last thing on your mind. Naj and Edward, that better *not* be a jar with a grass-hopper in it! Whatever it is, put it away right now. The pair who comes up with the best project in the class will get a prize."

"What kind of prize?" Terry asked.

"Hand up next time, please, Terry. The prize will be a bag full of goodies."

"What kind of goodies?" Kevin asked.

"What does it matter?" Ms. Pria snapped.

"Well, we have to decide if it's worth doing a good job, don't we?" Chris said.

"This project is not optional, Chris. And I'd really like to see something more than a blank piece of paper with your name on it this time."

"Can I hand in a blank piece of paper with my name *and* my partner's name on it?"

The class laughed.

"Chris! You will have detention today during lunch. I've had just about enough of your back talk for one day!"

Chris grinned, as happy as if he'd just received a student of the year award.

Bethany raised her hand. "What does the project have to be about, Ms. Pria?"

"It must address recycling, reusing, or waste."

Bethany squealed. She had the same look of joy you see on people's faces when they win a game show on TV.

Of course, Chris couldn't resist and yelled out, "What if we recycle Bethany? We could use her as a garbage can at the front of the school, and everybody can throw their empty cans and bottles at her. She'd love that!"

He started laughing hysterically at his own joke, and some of the other kids joined him.

Before Ms. Pria could scream at him or send

him to the principal's office, Emily yelled out, "Chris, if there is anybody in this entire school who is the very definition of a garbage can it would be *you*. Nobody is interested in hearing your voice right now."

Ms. Pria beamed at Emily. "Thank you, Emily. You took the words right out of my mouth. Chris, you will be spending lunchtime in detention all week."

Chris was still looking shocked that Emily, who'd barely spoken to him since she'd started school, had just had the guts to tell him off in front of the entire class. People started giggling and laughing *at* Chris, although they stopped as soon as he locked his menacing eyes on theirs.

When the lunch bell rang, some of the kids went up to Emily and patted her on the back, winked, or smiled at her. I was furious. She was becoming even more popular! I was the one who usually told Chris off. Everybody looked to *me* to rescue them when he stepped out of line. And now here was Emily taking over!

I was throwing my books into my bag when Tanya asked me if she could pair up with me.

I agreed. I was secretly hoping I'd find her a best friend and beat Emily before then, but I was willing to help her out in the meantime.

As we were walking out of the classroom I noticed Emily and Bethany approach Ms. Pria. I bent down and pretended to tie my shoelace. Emily and Bethany were whispering excitedly, but I couldn't hear what they were saying. Then Ms. Pria clapped her hands and said, "What a wonderful idea, girls!"

I was desperate to know what was going on.

Rules for Friendship Formations—Trios

Forming a trio must always be avoided. BUT if you are in a situation where you have NO CHOICE (it must be a serious case of no choice, equivalent to, say, "I was stuck on a desert island and had no choice but to eat a scorpion") then here are some survival tactics.

1. Always try and sit in the middle of the trio so you can control the conversation. If you're on the side then the others could ignore you.

2. Remember that the friendship is never equally divided. There is a pair in every trio. One person will always feel left out of the special magic between the other two.

3. Try and give equal attention to both other friends.
4. Be on the lookout for a new friend just in case you're the one in danger of falling off.

Chapter 14

I spotted Lucy in the lunch line. I grabbed Tanya's hand and practically dragged her along behind me.

"I'm scared, Lara," she said, her voice all wobbly.

"There's nothing to be scared of, Tanya. Bungee Jump Friend is the ultimate rush. It will come so naturally, you'll see. I really can't understand why you insist on acting so shy with everybody else. *We* can talk for ages. So have confidence in yourself. You actually *do* have something to say to people."

I was proud of myself. My pep talks were getting better each day.

Just then we were stopped by Juanita and

Nora from the sixth grade. I'd helped them out before the summer.

"Lara!" Juanita cried. "We need your help!"

"Can't it wait?" I asked, nervously watching the lunch line getting shorter.

"No, it can't," Nora wailed. "We ditched Sarah, and now she's sending us notes about how we've broken her heart and ruined her life. What do we do?"

I remembered the situation. It had been tricky, and I'd been reluctant to provide my services. I'd guessed from the moment they came to me that Sarah was the third wheel. But *nooooo*, they had insisted they were friends for life. It was a typically messy trio problem.

"I'm busy now," I said impatiently.

"But she isn't taking the hint. We don't want to be friends with her anymore."

"*Then she's better off without you!*" I shrieked.

It was as though I'd slapped them in the face. Even Tanya flinched.

I grabbed Tanya's hand and took off, trying to control my breathing as we rushed to the line.

I couldn't let myself think about the

consequences of my hysterical outburst. If Nora and Juanita blabbed to the rest of the school, my reputation as the Friendship Matchmaker who *never* takes sides, who listens to *all* parties involved, would be flushed down the toilet.

My head hurt. It had been an emotionally exhausting start to the year.

By the time we arrived at the lunch line Lucy was paying for her food. We hovered off to the side and, when she turned around with her tray in her hand, I pounced, pushing Tanya ahead of me.

Except I pushed a little too hard.

Tanya collided with Lucy, sending Lucy's chicken potpie flying down Lucy's shirt to land in a splattered, messy heap on the ground.

Lucy, with sauce and meat dripping down her top, looked slightly dazed and confused.

Tanya looked like she was going to burst into tears. "I'm . . . so sorry, Lucy," she whispered.

"It's not your fault, Tanya," I said. "*I* pushed you. *I'm* the clumsy one. How about you go with Lucy to the bathroom and help

105

her clean up? Lucy, I'll get you another chicken potpie."

"Um . . . okay . . ."

"You're going . . . ?" Tanya whispered, her eyes wide with panic.

She was frozen to the spot. How was I going to have a chance at finding her a best friend if she couldn't even handle a situation where *I* was the one who looked like the idiot?

But I wasn't giving up.

"You'll be fine," I said through gritted teeth. "You are a *great person*. Keep telling yourself that."

Lucy was too busy flicking bits of meat off her top with a napkin to notice our whispering.

I pushed them away in the direction of the bathroom and joined the lunch line.

I wondered if Emily was having as much trouble as I was. Maybe it had been a mistake to choose one of my top five Total Loners for the challenge. There was so much at stake, and here was Tanya practically hyperventilating at the thought of talking to Lucy without me as a buffer.

To be honest I just wanted to lie down in the nurse's office until the bell rang for us to go home.

But you don't earn Potts County Middle School's official Friendship Matchmaker title by being a quitter.

I waited outside the girls' bathroom with a new chicken potpie for Lucy. I also got some red licorice, as it turns out Tanya and I both love it.

I was hoping to hear Lucy and Tanya in a flurry of conversation. If Tanya was really thinking, she could have started it all off by talking about how clumsy I was. They could have had a laugh at my expense; I wouldn't have minded at all. They could have used me as a point of unity. Lots of friendships start out that way. They were lucky I had such an understanding, compassionate heart and that I wouldn't have been upset by it. These are the sacrifices I am willing to make in my quest to help others.

But all I heard was a deafening silence.

I didn't want to go inside with food, so I called out, "Tanya? Lucy? Are you there?"

Nothing.

I tried again.

"They're not here," said a voice. And out stepped Emily.

I almost dropped the potpie.

"What are you doing here?" I asked, which I admit was a stupid question because you don't have to be a genius to figure out why somebody would need the bathroom.

The same thought must have crossed Emily's mind because she ignored my question. "Lucy's gone to the basketball courts, and I saw Tanya walk off alone toward the playground."

I couldn't be sure, but it seemed to me that she emphasized the word "alone."

"Tanya seemed pretty upset. Almost crying. Is everything okay?"

"Everything is perfectly fine, thank you very much! I don't need you snooping around just so you can find out how I'm doing with Tanya. I don't see Bethany paired up with anybody yet. She's still a To—"

I stopped myself just in time. Nobody, least of all Emily, needed to know about my Total Loner list.

"I don't know why you're acting so crazy," Emily said. "I'm just worried about Tanya. She seemed really upset."

"Oh, please. You're probably happy to see her like that. Well, this competition isn't over yet!"

I spun on my heel and stormed off before Emily had a chance to respond. What nerve she had! Gloating like that while Tanya was upset somewhere and Lucy was walking around smelling like meat and gravy.

I raced to the basketball courts and found Lucy. "Here's a new chicken potpie," I said. "Sorry again. Remember, it was all *my* fault, not Tanya's. I'm sure you can both still be good friends."

"She's weird," Lucy said, taking a bite out of the pie. With her mouth full, she continued, "I joked that you must have two left feet, but she got all defensive and said *she* was the one who'd lost her balance. Then she just left. Said she wanted to see her little brother. Thanks for the pie!"

How could I work my magic when Tanya was sabotaging my efforts to help her? She was her own worst enemy! I couldn't understand what the problem was. Lucy was now definitely off the list as potential BF material. That left only Stephanie, the talkaholic.

I walked over to the elementary school playground and saw Tanya in the sandbox with her brother. The bell rang and they hugged forever and then blew each other kisses.

Chris could have a field day with this display of affection! It's not like they weren't going to see each other right after school. I sighed. Tanya was a more troublesome case than I'd first thought.

When I asked Tanya what happened, she shrugged and said she didn't want to talk about it. Then she was silent again until the bell rang to go home.

Chapter 15

One of the biggest sacrifices I have had to make as the official Friendship Matchmaker is not having my own friends. Like I said, with my busy schedule at school helping others, I am a Loner by Choice.

But that doesn't make weekends very much fun.

It was a really hot Saturday. In an ideal world—not that I was dreaming, not that I was giving much thought to this—my best friend would be over and we'd be swimming in my pool, tossing the beach ball. Mom would yell at us to come and eat lunch, and we'd wrap ourselves in our towels and sit on the trampoline eating our hot dogs with extra ketchup and sharing a greasy plate of home-made french fries with heaps of salt. Then we'd jump back in the pool, ignoring Mom's twenty-minute rule, and swim until our skin was all crinkly and we'd had enough.

Not that I was dreaming.

Instead, I was swimming alone.

My sister, Tara, thought she was too cool to hang out with me and was at the local pool swimming with her friends. Mom and Dad had yelled at her for being selfish, but she'd just yelled right back. "You're the ones who came up with the bright idea of a five-and-a-half-year age difference. *I'm* not the selfish one."

That had gotten Mom started about work commitments and late nights up dealing with colic and how hard it had all been. So I ended up hanging out in the pool wondering whether I was an accident and what I could steal from Tara's room as punishment for leaving me behind while she had fun with her friends.

Then the phone rang and Dad yelled out that it was for me.

"Who is it?" I yelled back, because I was

sure it must have been a prank. Loners by Choice generally don't get phone calls.

"A girl named Tanya. From school."

I raced up the pool stairs, quickly dried off, and took the cordless phone from my dad.

"Hi, Tanya! How are you?"

I realized I was gushing and quickly adjusted my tone. As Friendship Matchmaker I had to maintain a certain level of composure.

Tanya said, "I just wanted to say sorry for yesterday. I made a mess of the whole thing."

I leaned back in a banana chair, wriggling my toes in the hot sun. "That's okay. It was my fault, launching you at Lucy like that. I got a little carried away and pushed you too hard. If things had gone according to plan you would have done beautifully, I just know it."

She obviously wanted to avoid the topic because she said, "So what are you doing today? It's really hot, isn't it?"

"Yeah, it's boiling! I'm just hanging out at home. We have a pool."

"I'm sitting in front of a fan eating ice. Our

AC's broken. Guess what my dad got me? *The Curse of Shark Island* on DVD!"

"No way!" It was the film version of one of our favorite books.

"Do you . . . I mean, I understand you have a Rule against mixing with people outside of school . . ."

"How do you know?"

"I heard you explaining your Rules when you made your announcement a while ago about being the school's Friendship Matchmaker."

"Oh . . . yeah."

"I totally understand why you'd have to set that Rule . . . obviously you need to keep, like, a professional gap between the rest of us and yourself or things could get all messed up."

"Do you want to come over and watch *The Curse of Shark Island* at my place?" I offered.

"*Really?*"

"Our air conditioner works fine and we can go swimming afterward. I can break the Rule this one time. Anyway, it's still a professional meeting. We can go through a Bungee Jump Friend practice run. We can role play. I'll be

Stephanie. So, really, I'm not even breaking my Rules. If anybody finds out I'll just say I give weekend sessions to special people."

"Oh, thanks, Lara! I'll ask my dad. I'm sure he won't mind dropping me off."

Tanya arrived within half an hour. I was impressed that she'd abandoned her home-made animal tops and weird track pants. She was wearing denim shorts and a T-shirt and her frizzy hair was pulled back in a braid. She was definitely improving and had obviously been paying attention to my Fashion Rules. (I'd laminated a copy and ordered her to stick it on her bedroom closet door to study each night.)

Mom made us microwave popcorn. She also made us smoothies with crushed ice and put little umbrellas in our glasses. We sat in the living room, drew all the blinds, and watched the movie in the dark, turning the volume up really loud so we felt like we were in a movie theater.

Tanya had brought her bathing suit. After the movie—which we both thought should be

compulsory viewing for the entire universe—
we jumped into the pool. As we were throwing
the beach ball to each other I realized I had
to slip into my Friendship Matchmaker role
for a little while. I had my professional duties
and integrity to think about—not to mention
helping Tanya in my mission to find her a best
friend. It impressed me, the way I was able to
always think about the greater good.

"Okay, so let's do a role-playing activity.
I'll be Stephanie and you can be yourself."
I giggled. "*Obviously*. Let me set the scene:
Drama with Ms. Fraser."

"I hate drama."

"Well, that doesn't really matter because it's
just an example. Okay, so we're in class waiting
our turn to act as the president or a talking
robot or a doctor saving a life with kitchen
utensils, or whatever Ms. Fraser's cooked up
for us to do. So you're standing next to me,
Stephanie, when you say . . ."

I waved at her, motioning for her to take her
cue.

"Um . . . *Doctor* Stephanie, are you sure

stopping the patient's blood flow with Saran Wrap is the best option?"

"Good point, Nurse Tanya! What do you think about me performing open heart surgery with a whisk and barbecue tongs?"

"A fine idea, Doctor! Only remember to clean the ketchup off the tongs! We don't want to confuse Heinz with a leaking blood vessel!"

We got the giggles, climbed out of the pool, and spread out on the banana chairs, letting the hot sun dry us off. We were still laughing hysterically when Tanya's dad picked her up an hour later.

Chapter 16

On Monday morning before school I was in the reception area outside the staff room waiting to see Mr. Smith. I needed to borrow some lunch money, since I'd forgotten mine. The bell on top of the door jingled, and I looked over to see Emily coming in. There was only a small couch, so she had no choice but to sit next to me. She leaned back and folded her arms across her chest, stretching her legs out in front of her. I took a close look at her outfit. She was obviously in the mood for looking like a zebra: black-and-white-striped T-shirt, black skirt with a thick white hem, black headband and white hair tie, and one black and one white earring. Plus black shoes and white socks.

"Is it International Save the Zebra Day?" I asked.

She smoothed out her skirt. "Thanks," she said enthusiastically. "I agree, I do look great."

What nerve!

"You like making a statement with your clothes, don't you?"

"Sure. Why not? It's fun."

"On weekends, maybe. But it's risky at school."

"Are black stripes against your Rules?"

"Not exactly. The zebra look never really crossed my mind. But it's just safer to dress in a way that isn't going to put you straight into the firing line of a bully. Is that such a bad thing?" I sat up nice and tall. "I'm only thinking of people's well-being."

"How about teaching kids to stand up to bullies instead of getting them to act like sheep?"

I sighed heavily. Emily had obviously watched too many Disney movies. "I am not saying people should be sheep. But if you're at war, isn't it better to dress in camouflage than run into battle in rainbow colors screaming 'come and get me'?"

She burst out laughing. "At war? You're so dramatic. This is *school*."

"Exactly my point."

She studied me carefully. "Well, we obviously see things differently." Then, under her breath she muttered, "Poor Tanya . . ."

"What did you say?"

"Nothing . . ."

I stared at her for a moment and then looked away.

"You know," she said, "one time at my elementary school this guy, Alex Lopez, called me names for being Chinese."

"That's horrible."

She flashed a defiant look at me. "So what would your Rules suggest I should have done, you know, about my ethnicity?"

"Um . . . nothing . . . you can't change your ethnicity."

"Exactly. And I shouldn't have to."

"But you can change other stuff about yourself—I mean, people *generally*, not you specifically, change stuff about themselves that *can* be changed."

Emily smirked. "I punched Alex in the face and tripped him in the hallway."

She obviously found my horrified expression amusing and laughed.

"So, are you in trouble?" she asked.

"No. I forgot my lunch money. I'm never in trouble."

"I was always getting into trouble at my old schools."

"Well, assault will do that to you."

She shrugged. "It was worth it. But I wasn't only getting into trouble for taking my revenge on kids who bullied me." She grinned. "In fourth grade I smuggled a kitten into class, and she climbed up onto the teacher's desk and peed on her notebook!"

I couldn't help but giggle. It was unacceptable of me, letting my guard down like that when we were in a serious competition, and, to top it all off, Emily would probably be considered a violent criminal in some states. I coughed, trying to cover my giggle.

"Are you in trouble again?" I eventually asked.

"Nah, not today. I just need to ask permission for something. Don't want them to go bonkers the way they did with the fund-raiser."

"What are you doing?"

"That's for me to know and you to find out."

I frowned. She was infuriating!

～

We had PE first period that day. We were going to play T-ball. Ms. Kozub picked Juan and Aidan as captains. They stood in front of the class and took turns choosing their teams. It's the most psychologically damaging part of school. I'm certain that serial killers and psychopaths were all probably picked last in sports.

Sure enough, people like Kevin, Tanya, and Bethany were ignored as Juan and Aidan called out their team members. Aidan picked me first, as I usually had a knack for helping to choose a winning team based on my knowledge of everybody's personalities, weaknesses, and strengths. Of course, I told him to choose Tanya, even though I knew she was terrible at T-ball.

Emily was still the new girl and therefore an unknown when it came to her sporting ability. So Juan and Aidan were both avoiding picking her. But she didn't look stressed. Bethany was biting her nails anxiously. Kevin's eyes darted between Juan and Aidan as they skipped over him. The other kids waiting to be called shifted nervously from one foot to the other. Emily whispered into Bethany's ear. Bethany raised an eyebrow in surprise but nodded.

Then the most peculiar thing happened. Bethany locked eyes with Aidan and shook her head and waved her hands as if to say "don't pick me." Aidan looked confused. Then, when it was Juan's turn, Bethany locked eyes with him and also shook her head and waved her hands. Juan looked stumped and you could sense him hesitating. Then he called out Kevin. It was now Aidan's turn, and Bethany started waving and shaking her head again, as though being picked by Aidan was the last thing she wanted. He shrugged and, for no explicable reason, called out her name. She marched over and joined us. Emily was looking at Bethany and grinning from ear to ear.

It was a beautifully executed plan, and I was insanely jealous for not having thought of it before.

Emily was picked last, so she joined our team.

She sauntered over and winked at me. "See, we've all got our little tricks for helping others fit in!"

I was furious. Was she trying to steal my title? Take my place? Kick me out? Push me from being an LBC to a TL?

"It was a fluke," I snapped and turned my back on her.

We all dispersed into our positions. Bethany bounded up to me as we waited for the game to start. Standing inches from my face (definitely cornflakes for breakfast with banana and soy milk) she said: "It was amazing to be picked! Usually I'm one of the last kids standing. And Aidan didn't even look like it hurt to call out my name! It's so good to be playing outdoors in the fresh air. Think of how much electricity we're saving not being in the classroom with the lights and fans on."

"Yeah, good point. Are you and Emily planning something?"

"Yes."

"What?"

She wagged her finger in front of me. "Not telling!"

"What did you do at recess on Friday?"

"Read in the library."

"With Emily?"

"Nope. Alone."

"What about lunchtime?"

"Kept Mr. Smith company on recess duty. I walked around with him. He has some great ideas for reducing global warming. It was fascinating."

So Emily hadn't found Bethany a best friend yet. That meant I still had a chance of winning and keeping my reputation.

The day suddenly looked ten times brighter.

"Why were you writing notes in class about Samuel?" I asked Alan as we stood in the sixth-grade locker area at the end of recess. Samuel had requested an emergency intervention session before the bell rang.

"It was no big deal . . ."

"Well, it obviously was to Samuel. You hurt his feelings." I put a hand on his shoulder. "Would you like it if Samuel backstabbed you *in writing*?"

"I didn't know he saw me and Josh passing notes."

"That's not the point, Alan."

Tanya walked up and stood beside me, watching me in Friendship Matchmaker mode. When I'd finished, and Alan had apologized to Samuel and they agreed they were best friends again (I made them sign a No Backstabbing Agreement), Tanya and I headed to the seventh-grade locker area.

"Bungee Jump Friend with Stephanie will take place during lunchtime today," I said.

"Okay . . ."

"I promise you there is no need to be nervous. Do you trust me?"

"Yes," she said without hesitation. "Watching you just now, it's obvious you're an expert."

"There you go! I know you have all it takes to be true best-friend material. So let Stephanie see what a great personality you have—following my Rules of course—and you'll be best friends in no time."

～

Stephanie was near the water fountain talking to her older sister, Stacey. I waited within hearing distance and nudged Tanya forward.

"Hi, Stephanie," Tanya said nervously.

But Stephanie was too busy arguing with Stacey to notice Tanya.

"But you promised you'd let me come with you," Stephanie said. "And Mom said you had to take me."

"I'm really sorry, Stephanie. I promise I am. But Yas said no siblings allowed. It's her party. I can't tell her who to invite."

"But that's not fair! You know how much I love bowling."

"It's not up to me, Stephanie! Get over it!"

Stacey gave Stephanie a quick pat on the shoulder and walked off.

"Retreat," I whispered to Tanya. "Retreat!"

Tanya looked back and, noticing me wildly thrashing my arms around, beckoning her to come back, she ran over.

"What's wrong?"

"Nobody could Bungee Jump safely into that! She's too upset about her sister. We'll have to find another time when she's in the right mood."

I ignored Tanya's wide smile, not wanting to read too much into her enthusiasm for the delay. After all, what chance did I have of finding Tanya a friend if she didn't want to go along with my mission? I stuffed the thought right in the back of my mind, not wanting to dwell on it.

Ms. Pria let us spend the afternoon working on our Save the Planet Day projects.

"Remember, class, your project needs to be fun and informative. You need to be teaching others about recycling and ways to protect the planet. Chris, would you kindly return to the world of the living and stop dozing off in my class? Claire and Jemma, am I to actually believe that your project is simply a list of global warming websites?"

"Well, yeah," Jemma said. "We're giving people ideas on what to read and stuff."

Ms. Pria snatched the piece of paper and folded it in half. Then she started fanning her face.

"The only use this paper has to the planet is as a homemade fan. Start again. And this time, put in some effort, please."

Tanya and I had decided to do a poster with a large painting in the middle and facts and figures on the sides. We drew the earth wearing sunglasses, a tank top, and flip-flops, with a speech bubble that read, "Turn the heat down! I'm hot!" We used acrylic paints to make it colorful. Then we typed out recycling tips and stuck them on the rest of the poster.

Ms. Pria walked past and smiled. "Now, class, this is what I call an excellent effort. Well done, Lara and Tanya! You make a great pair!"

Tanya blushed, and we grinned at each other.

I noticed Emily and Bethany were writing on a pad of paper. They weren't using any art or craft supplies or the computer. Whatever they had planned, it looked boring, and I felt silly for having been intimidated by their plans.

Chapter 17

"Good morning, everyone," Ms. Pria said, cradling her mug of tea as she stood at the front of the classroom on Wednesday. "Today is our school's Save the Planet Day. You're going to have the opportunity to demonstrate your wonderful projects to the class. The best project will win the prize!"

Everyone took turns standing up in front of the class to show their work.

When it was our turn, Tanya and I presented our poster. It was so big we both had to hold it up. Tanya had come to my house after school the day before to finish it. Instead of drawing the sunglasses, we'd found an old pair of real sunglasses and stuck them on. We'd also glued a newborn baby's onesie on the earth. As modest as I am, I had to admit the poster was fantastic. I was sure we would take home the prize. Ms. Pria made everybody give us a round of applause.

Emily and Bethany were last. They stood up in front of the class. But they were empty-handed. They looked at Ms. Pria and she nodded. "Go ahead, girls," she said.

"What's going on?" Tanya whispered to me.

I shrugged, as intrigued as she was.

"Hi," Emily began. "For our project we need everybody to follow us to the basketball court."

There was an eruption of excited voices as we filed out of the classroom and made our way to the basketball court. Ms. Pria walked with us, yelling out orders to stay in two lines and to keep our voices down because it was still class time. With each step, I felt more anxious. What did Emily and Bethany have up their sleeves? And, more important, would it be better than our project?

When we arrived at the basketball court my

heart sank. There were three big cardboard boxes painted red, green, and yellow spaced at various distances from the free-throw line of the court. The first box was labeled Reuse, the second box Recycle, and the last box Discard.

Two large boxes were at center court.

Emily and Bethany stood next to Ms. Pria, who shouted at us to all be quiet and then nodded and beckoned to Emily and Bethany to take over.

"Okay, we need you to form two lines," Bethany commanded, "one behind each box at center court."

"What nerdy thing have you got planned for us, Bethany?" Chris taunted as we all shuffled along and divided up behind the boxes.

"Ah, let it go, will you, Chris?" Jemma yelled. "This beats being in class any day!"

"Definitely!" somebody said.

"It's unreal!"

"If you don't want to play with us, Chris," Bethany called out, "you can always wait for us in the classroom."

"Ooh!"

"Go, Bethany!"

I couldn't believe my ears. Bethany had never dared to talk back to Chris before. What had Emily done to her?

"Nah," Chris said with a casual shrug. "I want to see what this is all about."

"It's a recycling relay," Bethany explained. "Each team has a box of garbage. Don't worry, it's all clean. You have to take an item and then run to the three boxes and decide which box it belongs to: Reuse, Recycle, or Discard."

"Reusing is the cheapest option," Emily said. "It uses fewer resources. Recycling is the second-best option. Discarding or landfilling is the least-best option."

"The winner is the team who has the most items in the correct boxes. We've got a stopwatch too. So remember, it's a race!"

There was another buzz of excitement through the class. Everybody was pumped up to play. I overheard people's comments:

"It must have been Bethany's idea. She's the one who's so into the environment. It's awesome!"

"Wow, I never even thought about reusing stuff. I hope I know which box to put it in! What a cool idea!"

"What a smart project," Tanya said to me.

"Yes, smart," I said through clenched teeth.

Needless to say, the relay was a massive success and Emily and Bethany won the prize.

I wanted to curl up somewhere and hide from Emily. Did she think I didn't notice her smug grin? That self-congratulatory expression on her face?

Bethany was surrounded by a group of kids patting her on the back and congratulating her. They didn't even seem to mind her close-talking. Even Chris joined in and asked Ms. Pria if Bethany could take over class from now on so we could run math and science relays too.

Bethany suddenly locked eyes with me and bounded over.

"What did you think, Lara?" she cried excitedly.

"It was great," I said, trying to sound enthusiastic.

"It was my idea but I would never have been

able to do it if Emily hadn't encouraged me. I remember in our first induction session you told me I shouldn't do or say anything that would make me look like an environment nut, so I wasn't sure, but Emily told me to take a chance. And look! It worked!"

Just then Claire and Jemma grabbed Bethany's hand and led her away. Emily joined them and they walked together back to class, laughing and joking. And when Emily left them to go to the bathroom, Claire and Jemma walked on with Bethany as if they'd all been the best of friends forever.

Meanwhile, Tanya started chewing on a pen as we walked, and I couldn't tell if it was a sign of regression or whether she was having second thoughts about my ability to find her a best friend.

Because I hated to admit that I was.

Chapter 18

"Good morning, Lara, marinara," Omar said as I walked into class the next day.

"Hey, Omar," I answered flatly. I wasn't in the best of moods. I'd just seen Claire, Jemma, Emily, and Bethany huddled together and laughing like hysterical hyenas.

"I overheard Ms. Pria telling Mr. Laidlaw that she'd just made some copies of a quiz, whiz. She's testing us on last week's geography class, pass. What a bummer, dumber."

A quiz. Great. Just what I needed.

Tanya emerged from down the hall, followed by Chris.

"Hey, Electric Shock, didn't you have time to fix your hair today?"

He was right. Tanya's hair was all over the place. She looked miserable and was obviously trying to ignore Chris.

Then I gasped. Tanya was wearing a T-shirt with a sewn-on koala. I sighed and slowly shook my head. Regression was sometimes a problem with my clients. But it was my own failure if a client I was working with on a one-on-one basis was going back to old habits.

I really was very considerate. Not for a second (okay, not for ten to twenty seconds) did I blame Tanya. She had issues. That's why she was a Total Loner and I was the Friendship Matchmaker. I had to work with the TLs and help them, not blame them for their obvious problems. So she was having an "I love koalas" setback. And she'd run out of styling mousse. That was easily fixed. I'd ignore it for now and intervene when the time was right. Besides, there was Chris to deal with.

"And what's with that dumb T-shirt?" he barked. "You look like a tour guide at the zoo."

"Ew!" I cried, loud enough for the other kids that were gathering to hear. "Chris, you stink! Didn't you shower this morning?"

"I can't smell anything, sing," Omar said, sniffing the air. "Oh, well, maybe . . . yeah, there's a slight whiff, myth."

"It isn't me!" Chris pleaded.

"Why don't you leave Tanya alone and go and make friends with a bar of soap," I snapped. "You'd do us all a favor if you smelled halfway decent before class starts."

Actually, he smelled fine. But since when did there have to be any truth in teasing? It was working. Some kids were snickering and pointing at him. He stormed past me, shoving my shoulder as he passed.

"Get outta my way, fatso," he said.

It was pretty lame given I was skinny and *he'd* banged into *me*.

Chris got his revenge in class later that morning when we were taking the geography quiz.

Ms. Pria had made me sit next to Omar. She'd put Tanya beside Bethany, at the table directly in front of Chris.

When Ms. Pria was pretending to look for a tissue in her bag but really texting (who did she think she was kidding?), I heard Chris hissing at Tanya to lift up her paper so he could cheat.

Tanya tried to ignore him, but when he kicked her chair she slowly lifted her paper and let him copy.

I wished I was sitting closer so that I could have done something to help her.

But Tanya had only finished page one of the quiz. Chris was getting impatient and turned his attention to Bethany. He started hissing at her too and throwing tiny bits of chewed paper at the back of her head.

Bethany was even worse than Tanya. She actually wrote out the answers, scrunched the piece of paper up and threw it back to Chris. Ms. Pria, meanwhile, was still texting, only occasionally glancing up.

It was sad the way they both gave in to Chris like that.

When we finished our quizzes Ms. Pria collected them and gave us reading time while she marked them. We cheered. Reading time was so much fun. We were allowed to sit anywhere in class with a book and read.

Of course, with Ms. Pria concentrating on correcting our quizzes, it meant we could sit anywhere in class with a book and *talk*.

Tanya was still in a mood and declined my offer to hide behind the bookshelf so we could chat about our next Bungee Jump attempt.

"Do you mind if I just read?" she asked. "Maybe we can talk about it tomorrow. I'm not really in the mood today. Sorry, Lara."

I didn't have the heart to be angry with her so I let it go. She took a book out of her bag and sat down by herself in a corner of the classroom to read. She was obviously having a strange day, what with the frizz, koala, and solitary reading.

I noticed Bethany, Jemma, and Claire sitting close together against the back wall, out of view of Ms. Pria, deep in conversation.

How had they become so close, so quickly? The only consolation I had was that they were a trio. As long as they remained a trio, I still had a shot at winning. Jemma and Claire would soon leave Bethany out. It was a scientific fact and just a matter of time.

Emily was sitting on one of our classroom beanbags. Her lap was filled with booklets. I found myself slowly approaching her and then sitting down on the floor a short distance away.

"What are you reading?" I asked, curious.

"Instruction manuals," she answered, holding one up for me to see.

It was a manual for assembling what looked like a coffee table.

"Why?"

She shrugged. "I'm just trying to figure out what to do when I'm older. I'm looking at traditional and nontraditional jobs. So I figured somebody obviously writes these manuals. I'm just wondering if I'd be interested in instructing people on how to put together an eight-piece table setting."

I must have looked baffled because she said, "With my brains, people always say, 'That girl will be a doctor or lawyer one day.' But I'm not interested in being what other people want me to be."

"So you want to write manuals for Ikea?"

She shifted in the beanbag. "Well, not

specifically Ikea. I imagine any furniture shop will do. But I guess if you can figure out an Ikea one, you can figure out any other one. Well, at least that's what my dad said in between swearing when he put together my new bed last night."

She went back to reading. I tucked my feet under me and tried not to stare at her.

"I paired up Jemma and Claire, you know," I said casually.

"That's nice," she said without looking up.

"It's not often you come across perfect matches. But they were. Same taste in clothes, music, TV shows, books. They even live on the same street."

"Interesting."

"You can't honestly expect that Bethany will last in a trio with them."

Emily put down her manual. "I can't say. But they seem pretty comfortable together."

"We agreed it had to be genuine best-friend material. Not just some temporary thing."

"Yeah, I know," she said. "But they seem really happy. Jemma and Claire love animals, and Bethany's mom works at an animal shelter. Jemma's and Claire's parents said they can help out with the animals at the shelter on the weekends."

"Oh."

"Did you know Bethany and her family are animal activists too?"

I slowly shook my head.

"And that Jemma and Claire would love any chance to be around animals and look after them?"

"Well, yeah, of course I know they love animals. That was one of the reasons I paired them. The Golden Rule of Shared Interests, thank you very much."

Emily fought back a smile.

"What's so funny?" I demanded.

"Nothing . . . um, it's just that this picture of a bedside table looks like a lunch box. I'm not so sure I'm cut out for this kind of work. My drawings are too good for these manuals."

I eyed her suspiciously and then burst out. "You think my Friendship Matchmaker services are funny, don't you?"

"No," she said in that annoyingly calm voice of hers.

"You think it's all one big joke!"

"I never said that."

"That's how you act!"

"You're misunderstanding me then."

We were suddenly interrupted by Ms. Pria's booming voice. "Chris, a big fat zero! It's obvious you cheated."

"I didn't cheat, Ms. Pria!" Chris cried. "You're being unfair. Even when I get the answers right you yell at me!"

"Nobody who came up with the answers you gave on page two could have produced the correct answers on page one."

"Huh?"

"I'm pretty sure I did not teach you that Johannesburg is the capital of China or that Hungary is part of New Zealand. Every answer is more absurd than the next!"

Chris glared at Bethany, who was sniggering with Claire and Jemma. Emily was grinning quietly to herself. I glanced at Tanya. She locked eyes with me and shrugged.

Once again Bethany had humiliated Chris.

By lunchtime the news of Bethany's trick had traveled across the school.

I didn't know how much longer I could stand watching Bethany being patted on the back.

Bungee Jump Friend

It might seem scary. But it's not. Trust me. You have to believe in yourself and your ability to talk about random topics.

If you can succeed at Bungee Jump Friend you will never again feel nervous about starting conversations with strangers. Like when your mom runs into an old friend at the mall and you're stuck beside her wondering what to talk about with the other kid as the moms moan about the days when they had time to brush their hair and read the newspaper.

Practice in front of the mirror. Have a mental list of topics for Bungee Jump situations; for example, what flavor chip is missing from the grocery store? How many more school vacations

do you think we should have? Why are parents
so mean and refuse to give us an iPhone/DS/
iPod until we're in high school?
   YOU CAN DO THIS!

Chapter 19

I can't do this," Tanya moaned, pacing up and down in front of the library.

"Don't say that! You can talk to *me* for ages."

"That's different."

"No, it's not. If you want a best friend you have to open up more. Stop being so shy. A couple of weeks ago I would never have thought you could have a telephone conversation or hang out. You've surprised me! So now surprise Stephanie."

"But I'm so nervous."

She did look a little queasy, but I tried to ignore it.

"Stephanie is a talkaholic so it will be easy. Just follow her lead."

Tanya took a deep breath.

"Think calm thoughts. Then walk over to her and say hi as you sit down next to her. Ask how her week's been, what she's doing on the weekend. The conversation will flow from there."

Tanya nodded slowly, and I gently nudged her in Stephanie's direction.

Stephanie was sitting on a bench eating a bag of chips. She didn't have a lot of friends, because she talked so much most people got fed up trying to compete with her. But I figured that Stephanie and Tanya would be a good balance.

Tanya sat down next to Stephanie.

I made my way over toward them and stood a short distance away.

"Hi, Stephanie. How are you?"

Stephanie looked up and smiled brightly. "I'm good, Tanya. These chips are delicious, although I normally hate spicy flavors, these have a yummy kick to them. Not that I like spicy food, it makes my stomach feel funny, although I like some kinds of curry, and

Mom's always cooking Mexican but she leaves the chili on the side. How's your day been?"

I gulped nervously, wondering how Tanya would respond.

"Good."

I sighed. Belly flop bungee jump.

"That geography quiz was pretty hard yesterday. Chris's answers were so funny. Bethany sure has guts. I'd never be able to trick him like that. It's nice you're hanging out with Lara now. Lucky you, being friends with her. She tried to help me at the beginning of last year, but I could never stick to her conversation topics. I'm hopeless that way. Did you know we have a field trip to the aquarium on Monday? I'm so excited. What are you doing this weekend?"

I felt exhausted listening to Stephanie. Tanya looked bewildered but was about to answer when Stephanie jumped in again.

"We're going to the circus. It's near our house, although Dad says it will be boiling hot in the tent but Mom checked the weather and it should be fine and sunny although they said it might reach over one hundred degrees, which means we'll have to bring lots of bottles of water because Dad says the circus prices are a big fat rip-off and imagine paying four dollars for a bottle of water when you can bring one from home."

Tanya stood up. I really didn't blame her.

"Ah, nice talking to you, Stephanie. I just remembered I have to return a book to the library."

She hurried off and I followed her to the library.

"Lara, I hope you don't think I'm cruel, but as lovely as Stephanie is in small doses, I think I'd go crazy if she were my best friend."

"You're probably right, Tanya," I said.

I'd run out of options. All my potential best friends for Tanya had been disasters.

Was it possible that Emily was going to win our competition?

⁓

Mom stood in the doorway of my bedroom with the phone in her hand. It was Saturday morning, and I was lying on my bed, working on the final chapters of my Manual.

"Tanya is on the phone," she said with a grin. Then she placed her hand over the receiver. "I'm so happy you've found a friend, darling!"

She passed me the phone and walked out, still grinning.

I was offended by her comment. If she only knew that it was *my* decision not to have a best friend. If she only knew that I was making a sacrifice for the greater good. And anyway, this was probably a professional call. Tanya was my client. Honestly, moms could really miss the obvious at times.

"Hi, Tanya!" I said. "What's up?"

"I'm at Mom's today and she's offered to drop me off at the movies while she does some shopping. Do you want to come? There's a new movie out about a haunted mansion. I mean, if you're free and don't mind breaking your Rules, of course."

"Sure! I'd love to come." I stopped, realizing I sounded way too eager. I couldn't let her think I was so bored at home that I was waiting for a call like this. Being a Friendship Matchmaker had outside duties too. Like

153

perfecting my glossary. Or stealing Tara's fashion magazines so I could update my Fashion Rules.

"What time is the movie? I just need to check if I'm free. I'm preparing for a Fashion Rules seminar I'm running with the new fifth-grade kids on Monday."

"We have the field trip to the aquarium on Monday."

"Oh, yeah. Tuesday then."

"Mom wanted to drop me off around eleven."

"That's cool. I can work it into my schedule."

We shared a jumbo box of popcorn and sat at the back of the theater. We kept on talking through the previews and commercials until the movie started. We screamed at the same time, laughed at the same time, and covered our eyes at the same time. When it was over, Tanya's mom bought us lunch. We were so inspired by the movie that we decided to write our own script for a scary movie, set on a haunted plane. Once Harry Potter's publishers released my

Manual I'd be famous and Steven Spielberg would probably be interested in our plane movie. But I couldn't tell Tanya that just yet.

We spent lunch working out the characters and plot while Tanya's mom smiled at us, a dreamy expression on her face.

It was quite possibly one of the best Saturdays of my year. It felt good to let loose and speak about all kinds of banned topics with Tanya. I made it clear to her though that it was strictly because we were out of school.

"Always remember different Rules apply at school," I said, then went on to confide that I wished Ms. Pria would set us weekly creative writing exercises so that we could get more practice.

Tanya's mom dropped me off, and I was walking through the door when Dad said, "Hi, honey. What did you do today?"

"Went to the movies with a friend," I said automatically.

I went to bed that night and couldn't sleep. I tossed and turned. It hit me that I no longer saw Tanya as just my client.

I sat up in bed and punched the air.

I felt fabulous.

I wanted to jump up and down and do somersaults. We had so much in common. We clicked like seat belts. Who cares if I juggled my Friendship Matchmaker duties with having a best friend? I'd never been happier.

That's when it occurred to me that Emily hadn't won.

I'd found Tanya a best friend after all.

Me.

Rules for Field Trips

A school field trip is a chance to put most of the Rules I've taught you into practice.

1. There is a bus trip (see Bus Trip Rules).
2. There is lunchtime (see Rules on table shapes, smelly food).
3. There is a teacher shouting out orders (see Rules on interacting with teachers).
4. There are potential trio situations (see Rules on Friendship Formations).
5. There are opportunities to talk (study my Rules regarding topics to avoid in conversation).
6. Everyone gets dressed up (follow my Fashion Rules. No one is going to want to hang around a weirdo at school let alone outside school).

In summary, field trips can be lots of fun. But it will all depend on the bus ride. Make sure you plan it right so you're not left sitting alone or ditched by your friends. Your enjoyment of the rest of the field trip depends on it!

Chapter 20

I woke on Monday morning desperately excited about my plan. I was going to:

a) ask Tanya to be my best friend

b) tell Emily that our competition result was a tie

c) make an announcement to my clients that I'd be easing up on my Friendship Match-maker duties.

From now on all mediation sessions and seminars would take place at recess. After all, a girl needed time with her best friend during lunch.

But I didn't get a chance. As soon as we arrived at school Ms. Pria ushered us onto the bus waiting to take us to the aquarium. I asked

Tanya to sit next to me and she was thrilled. I noticed Claire and Jemma were deep in conversation while Bethany stood nervously to the side. I was willing to bet she was wondering if they'd get the back row or if she'd be forced to find another seat while they sat together.

Emily skipped up to them looking excited. She was wearing a white top with pictures of dolphins, sharks, and tropical fish all over it. Her shorts were blue. She had dangling shell earrings on and a bag that said in large print: I've Been to the Coral Reef.

She caught my eye and pointed to her top.

"In the spirit of our visit to the aquarium," she said and winked. "Acceptable?"

I nodded yes, trying to fight back a smile.

Tanya and I boarded and sat next to each other toward the back. Emily then leaped ahead of everybody and ran to the back row. "These seats are taken!" she hollered as kids tried to shove past her. When Bethany, Claire, and Jemma hopped on, Emily called out to them. Bethany couldn't have looked more relieved.

I still had no chance to talk to either Tanya or Emily, because Ms. Pria insisted on working out her lungs.

"Chris and anybody else who feels inclined to act like a hooligan, just remember I will be issuing back-to-back lunchtime detentions plus a year-long ban on all further field trips, including our school carnival day, if I see or hear *any* nonsense!"

She took half the trip to lecture us and the other half to hand out a multiple-choice exercise we had to do when we were at the aquarium.

I put it in my bag, tucking it under my Manual, which I'd brought with me. I didn't want to risk leaving it in my desk in case somebody got their hands on it.

Because there was no time to talk to Tanya or Emily I decided I'd approach them at the aquarium.

We started out in the reptile section. I was walking along with Emily, reading the information panels and trying to answer our multiple-choice questions. Bethany, Claire, and Jemma were together too, close behind us. Emily was grouped with Omar, Stephanie, and David. I wasn't sure how she was coping, what with Stephanie's rambles and Omar's rhyming. Luckily David was a pretty normal guy when he wasn't around his basketball (Ms. Pria had made him leave it on the bus).

Ms. Pria and the two other teachers she'd brought along with her for crowd control were hovering around.

We were trying to answer a question about the diet of a crocodile. The area was jam-packed with kids from other schools and normal visitors. Tanya squeezed between two people to get close to the information display. I dropped my bag on the floor and stared at the crocodile while I waited for her.

That's when I saw them through the glass on the other side of the huge tank.

My heart skipped a beat.

My hands started to go clammy.

Ellie Solomon and Vicky Zevgolis.

Their eyes locked with mine. To my horror, they started to wave and walk toward me. I couldn't let Tanya or anybody from school see. My past would be exposed! I raced to the next section and they followed me.

They planted themselves in my way, cornering me in the amphibian exhibit.

There was no escape from . . . my two ex–best friends.

From kindergarten to fifth grade, we'd been inseparable. If we had to break into pairs for schoolwork, we took turns so nobody was ever left out. We became experts at cutting lunches or chocolate bars into thirds. We always chose round tables. Our parents enrolled us in ballet lessons after school, and we had matching bags and tutus. We finished each other's sentences. We had the same dreams, whether it was getting the red crayon in kindergarten or finishing the same book series in fourth grade. We were truly the perfect trio. Each enjoying exactly 33.33 percent of the friendship.

But then Ellie's family moved to a street near Vicky's house over spring break, and we returned to school with the percentages truly ruined.

Slowly but surely I was left out. Ellie and Vicky played together on the weekend. They came to school on Monday referring to conversations I hadn't been a part of. They weren't so worried about taking turns for group work. And when Ellie's mom withdrew her from ballet, Vicky followed immediately. I was no longer enough to make her stay.

It was the day of our field trip to the zoo that it hit me hard. As we lined up for the bus, I panicked about the seating arrangements. We'd always made sure to get in line first to get the back seat. We'd never failed. But this time they lined up toward the end of the line, even letting others go ahead of them as they spoke about the computer games they'd played at Ellie's house on Saturday afternoon. By the time we boarded, the backseat was full. Ellie and Vicky headed for a two-seater, and I was left in the aisle, alone, confused, humiliated. All the seats were taken, so I ended up sitting next to the teacher.

I went home and swore I'd never let myself be put in that situation again. Slowly I started work on my Manual, a do-it-yourself guide to Making and Keeping friends. I tried to make sense of the Rules, understand how the playground worked. I listened to people's conversations, watched how kids interacted. I became a psychologist and tried to read people's minds.

I always thought Ellie and Vicky had ditched me because of something I had done or said. Maybe I wasn't cool enough for them anymore. Maybe my conversations were boring or I was wearing the wrong clothes. I was racked with doubt.

And then the best thing in my life happened.

Over summer break the local council changed the zoning maps, and Ellie and Vicky moved to another school.

The first day of sixth grade I came to school a new person. I was going to use my mistakes to help other kids so they'd never have to go through what I did.

The Friendship Matchmaker was born.

Chapter 21

And here were Ellie and Vicky now, crashing my aquarium field trip, bringing back painful memories.

I felt dizzy and shaken.

"How are you?!" Ellie squealed.

Vicky grabbed my arm. "We've missed you!"

For a second my heart skipped for joy. I'd dreamed of a happy reunion so many times. A chance to go back to how we'd been. But when I studied their faces, I realized how fake they were acting and remembered that not once had they called or e-mailed me.

"I'm great," I said meekly. "It's been the best year of school . . ."

"Imagine seeing our *best friend* again," Vicky cried in a high-pitched voice. "After all this time!"

Ellie smiled insincerely. "Vicky and I started ballet again. We have *so* much fun. They put us together in all the concerts. They treat us like we're twins."

Vicky giggled. "Well, that's not the first time people have said that about us."

"Are you still dancing?" Ellie asked, twirling a lock of hair around her finger.

"No," I replied, suddenly noticing they were wearing matching friendship bracelets.

"Remember how much fun the three of us used to have?" Vicky said dreamily. "Every year the teachers used to tell our parents that we couldn't be separated. Remember that, Lara?"

That's when I noticed Emily out of the corner of my eye. She was watching us, listening to every word. Knowing she was seeing all this somehow made it even worse.

I fought back tears. I wanted to run away.

"Hey, Lara," Ellie said. "Remember when

we all cried in third grade because they were going to put you in Mr. Lux's class and keep Ellie and me in with Ms. Hunter? Our parents came to the school and begged them to put us in Mr. Lux's class with you, and they did!"

"Yeah," I said softly. "I remember."

They kept on talking.

"Remember when we worked out that the first letter of our first names nearly spelled love?"

"Remember when we were all teddy-bear ballerinas at the holiday pageant?"

"Remember how we used to share our allowance and buy lollipops from the store?"

I couldn't take it any longer. "I've got to go back to my class," I said, and rushed off without saying good-bye.

I wanted to run to the bathroom and cry.

All of a sudden the aquarium seemed to have emptied out. Kids from our class were the only ones around, and the teachers were nowhere to be seen. But as I passed our group I heard a loud commotion. Chris was holding up a book and reading aloud from it. Some of the kids were roaring with laughter. I couldn't figure out what was happening.

That's when I saw Bethany, her face blotchy with tears. Claire and Jemma were comforting her. Tanya was beside them. She was hunched up, arms folded across her chest. She looked miserable.

I looked over at Chris. My bag was open at his feet. My body felt like lead as I realized what he was reading: "'But most of all she doesn't have anything to talk about. Just smiles or shrugs. Need to fill her head with conversation topics . . .' Oh, and then there's this about Bethany: 'A real hopeless case and really bordering on being promoted to number three on my Total Loner list, except Tanya's sniffing habits are freaky and scare people (which is a problem when you need to match a friend to her) and she doesn't talk (shy people are always hard to match).' This is *hysterical*!" He caught sight of me and waved. "Lara, you're a genius!"

I wanted a hole to open up under me. Bethany looked over, sniffling and wiping her nose with a crumpled tissue. Claire and Jemma were giving me dirty looks. And then Chris topped it all off.

"But wait, here's the best part! Even I get a mention: 'Note to self: Chris loves picking on Tanya. Need to work out how to get her out of his sights. (But honestly, sometimes you can understand why.)' Gold!"

Tanya winced. Our eyes met. Then she ran off, crying.

I couldn't move. I was fixed to the spot and having an out-of-body experience at the same time.

"How could you write such nasty stuff?" Claire spat.

"We thought you were here to help us," Jemma said with a glare.

David, Stephanie, and Kevin looked on. Judging from the expressions on their faces, I guessed Chris had read out loud what I'd written about them too.

"I . . . I . . ." My tongue felt fat and furry. I couldn't talk. I didn't even know what I could say in my defense.

Suddenly Emily stepped up beside me and threw her arm around my shoulder.

"Don't any of you *dare* judge Lara! If you hadn't noticed, she has put her whole life on hold for you and everybody else at school. Every single kid whining about this person not talking to them, or that person ignoring their e-mails, comes to her for help. It's any wonder she has time to eat with all the work she has helping you all out!"

I stared at her in disbelief.

"None of you can pretend you don't have those habits she wrote about. Yes, David, I've seen you talking to your basketball."

David looked embarrassed.

"As for you, Chris, going through people's bags is *not* an act of friendship! Bethany, as much as I love hanging out with you, I'd rather not see your tonsils when you talk to me, and not everybody wants to hear about global warming twenty-four-seven!"

To my surprise Claire and Jemma started nodding in agreement, although they still had their arms around Bethany.

"And Stephanie, you need to learn how to count to ten between each sentence. But guess what, everybody? In spite of all this, the only person who stuck up for you and tried to find you happiness at school was Lara! And now you're turning against her because Chris, who has a brain the size of my thumbnail, wants to stir up trouble. You should know better!"

"Hey! What did I do?" Chris said, throwing his hands up.

Emily leaped toward him, grabbed the Manual from his hands, and told him to shut up before she told Ms. Pria he'd tried to climb into the crocodile tank. "And you better believe I'd lie to get you in trouble, and don't think Ms. Pria wouldn't give me the benefit of the doubt over you."

Chris glared at Emily but didn't say anything. Then he hurried off before Emily kept her word.

The strangest thing happened next. David, Stephanie, and Kevin walked up to me.

"I'm not upset, Lara," David said.

"Yeah, me neither," Kevin added with a shrug.

"It's true," Stephanie said. "You were the only one who truly wanted to help me."

I smiled shyly at them. "Still, I'm sorry about what I wrote. It was pretty awful stuff when I think about it now."

Their smiles reassured me that all was forgiven. I then walked over to Bethany.

"Sorry, Bethany," I said softly. "I didn't mean to hurt your feelings."

She sniffed and then half smiled. "It's okay, Lara. You didn't say anything that wasn't true. I can't help it, though. That's just who I am. That's probably why you never found me a friend. I was just too hard."

"That was my fault, not yours," I said. "You've got Claire and Jemma now. You're popular. And you didn't have to change a thing about yourself. My Rules were wrong. You didn't need me to be happy."

I turned to Emily and gave her a grateful smile. She handed me my bag and Manual.

Ms. Pria suddenly appeared. "Why are

you all dawdling instead of finishing your multiple-choice questions? Come on! We haven't got all day."

The others dispersed, leaving Emily and me in front of Ms. Pria.

"Can I go to the bathroom?" I asked Ms. Pria.

"Fine, but you have to go in pairs."

I looked at Emily and she nodded.

Ms. Pria sent us off with a strong warning to return to the group as quickly as possible.

As I expected, we found Tanya crying in the bathroom. She'd locked herself in one of the stalls.

"Please open the door, Tanya," I pleaded. Emily stood next to me, looking worried.

"Go away," she said, and hiccuped.

"I'm an idiot, I know," I said. "I'm so sorry. Everything I wrote about you was wrong and stupid. It was before I knew you."

"But, Lara, you said I don't have anything to talk about," Tanya said from behind the stall door.

"I know, Tanya, and I'm sorry. Remember, this was before I got to know you."

"What kind of an excuse is that? You only make horrible assumptions about people when you don't know them? Isn't that why you're a Friendship Matchmaker? To help kids who get picked on and judged?"

Her words hit me hard, and I lowered my head in shame.

She opened the door. We took a step back to let her out. Her face was streaked with tears. I felt awful.

"But even when you got to know me, didn't you once wonder why I was so different at school from when I was with you?"

"I . . . I just thought you were shy at school . . . with other kids . . ."

She sighed. "Remember I told you I was writing a how-to manual as well?"

I nodded and she continued.

"It was actually a survival guide."

"Surviving what?" Emily asked.

"Divorce."

I couldn't believe it. I had no idea.

"My parents just separated, Lara," Tanya said softly. "Right before the summer. My brother and I are living with Mom. We're with Dad every weekend. It's . . . horrible. And it's so hard on my little brother. So when I come to school it's hard to be my normal self with everybody. Most days I just want to go to the library and cry in a corner."

I felt winded. If I'd been a teeny-weeny bit sensitive I wouldn't have missed it. I thought back to all the hints she'd dropped. Wanting to wear clothes her mom had made her. Going all quiet when we spoke about her parents. *Visiting* her dad to play basketball.

A Friendship Matchmaker was supposed to listen. To care about people's feelings and their stories. All I'd done was try to turn Tanya into a different person. I hadn't respected her, or bothered to care about what she was going through.

"Tanya, I don't know what to say. If it makes any difference, I came to school today to tell you that I was finished looking for a best friend for you. I was hoping you'd think of me as your best friend . . ." I stole a glance at Emily who smiled but didn't interrupt me. "I would understand now if I'm the last person in the world you would want to be friends with," I finished.

Tanya looked at me in surprise and then blew her nose. She didn't say anything for a while. When I didn't think I could take the silence anymore she finally spoke up.

"Can we talk about what we want, at school and out of school? No banned topics? No Fashion Rules or books-to-read guidelines?"

I held up my Manual in front of them. I flicked through it, skimming my Rules and advice. Emily was right. I'd been thinking of school in the worst possible way. I was teaching kids to trust no one, especially themselves. I made a sudden decision and rushed to the garbage can and dropped the Manual in it.

"Sorry, Harry Potter's publishers," I whispered.

Then I turned to Tanya. "No more Rules or lists," I said firmly.

The three of us grinned.

"So homemade T-shirts are allowed?" she asked coyly.

"Yeah, sure," I said cheerfully.

"But the school-supplies sniffing isn't coming back, is it?" Emily said worriedly.

"Only in times of high stress," Tanya joked. "You just can't imagine how good a ruler smells during history tests."

We laughed, and then Emily and I waited outside the bathroom while Tanya washed her face and tried to get her puffy eyes back to normal size.

"So," Emily said confidently, folding her arms across her chest, "looks like we have a tie."

"Yep," I said. "Everybody's a winner."

"We obviously have our individual talents. I bet if we went into this Friendship Match-making business together we could make this the best school in the world. Bully-free and without a lonely person in sight. We could write another Manual! Do speed-friendship sessions at lunchtime! Start an online Friendship Match-maker service on the school's website!"

"Whoa!" I cried, holding my hands up to stop her from continuing. "Believe me, it all sounds very tempting. But, for once, I'm going to take some time off and enjoy being a best friend. After all, I'm Potts County Middle School's Friendship Matchmaker. And I've just made the best match of my career."

acknowledgments

Thank you to Dyan Blacklock for giving me the chance to turn back time and become a middle schooler all over again! It's been a pleasure working with the team at Omnibus. Thank you, Gina Inverarity, for your meticulous editing. Thanks are also due to my wonderful agent, Sheila Drummond. Thanks, Sally Ahmed, for your advice and suggestions.